STRONG UNDERCURRENTS

Cal Bartley

Onion Custard Publishing Ltd

Strong Undercurrents
© 2015 Cal Bartley

The Author asserts the moral right to be identified as the author of this work.
All rights reserved. This book is protected under the copyright laws of the
United Kingdom. Any reproduction or other unauthorised use of the material
or artwork herein is prohibited without the express written permission of the
Author.

British Library Cataloguing in Publication Data.
A catalogue record for this book is available from the British Library.

Published in the United Kingdom by Onion Custard Publishing Ltd.
www.onioncustard.com
Twitter @onioncustard
Facebook.com/OnionCustardPublishing

Paperback format: ISBN: 9781909129887

First Edition: November, 2015
Category: Contemporary Women's Fiction

Contents

1

Clare & Nick

Clare lay in bed with her eyes closed, wondering what was wrong. Her eyes were refusing to open. She considered what the problem might be. Then she realised – she had the hangover from hell. She and her friend Brigitte were only moderate drinkers, but last night they had both drunk more than usual to welcome in the New Year. She had another go at lifting her eyelids and regretted it immediately. Bright shafts of daylight darted arrows of pain into the back of her eyes. She screwed them shut with a groan of pain.

Clare wondered what time it was. She turned slowly onto her side, but the contents of her stomach didn't synchronise with the rest of her, and she felt as though she might throw up. She groaned again. Her husband, Nick, stirred.

"Wassa time?" he mumbled from the other side of the bed.

With great trepidation she opened her eyes again and focussed on the clock-radio. It read 09:59. As she watched, bleary-eyed, the numbers magically transformed to 10:00.

"Ten," she whispered, then added, "I don't feel well."

Nick grinned and said, "Well, you know what the cure for that is…" He started to stroke her back.

"No," she yelped. "Seriously, Nick, if I had sex I think I might actually die."

He sighed and stood up, stretching his rangy limbs and admiring his fit torso in the mirror. He ran a hand through his tousled blond hair. *What a wasted opportunity.*

He knew when he wasn't going to get anywhere. He padded to the bathroom, and came back with two painkillers and a glass of water.

"Here. Drink these and stay there. We've still got a couple of hours before we have to go to John and Brigitte's."

Clare did as she was told, then lay back on her pillow. Fragments of last night's party drifted slowly across her consciousness. New Year's Eve had taken the usual format of a moveable feast, held in one of the larger old houses in the Abingdon area. Last night's party had been hosted by Daphne and Marcus, with adults in the lounge and children filtering off to the TV room. At midnight they had all stood together and sung *Old Lang Syne*, as the older children took advantage of their tipsy parents and wheedled some champagne to toast the New Year. The children then returned to their TV and music, leaving the adults to continue chatting, and dancing. For some, it meant making a move back to the booze, and to re-focus on drinking as the main activity of their night.

Today's get-together was being held in Brigitte and John's home, as was the tradition on New Year's Day. The Taylor family were due to turn up from midday, and Clare had said she would bring a pudding. She drifted back to sleep, fretting about catering. Nick woke her up an hour later with a cup of tea.

"Come on, you," he said, sitting on the bed and gently stroking her shoulder. "You might want time to come round. I've brought you a strong cup of builders'."

Clare opened her eyes – the light wasn't so painful now. She sat up and sipped at her tea, slowly trying to piece together the previous evening.

"What time did we leave the party?" she asked groggily.

"Oh, around one," he answered vaguely. "Not really sure."

She thought back. She remembered leaving without

the children, as the three of them were sleeping with friends or cousins. The party was only two roads away, so she and Nick had happily staggered back. She vaguely remembered arriving home and, just as they got in, Nick had sworn, "Damn, I've left my phone. I'll have to go back and get it."

"Oh, leave it 'til the morning," Clare had said woozily. "Daph or Marcus can bring it with them tomorrow."

"You know I hate being without it, in case work phone. I'll just run back…" and with that he'd been out of the door without waiting for a reply. Clare had shrugged and carefully climbed the stairs to bed.

"Did you find your phone?" she asked now, remembering his exit.

"What?" There was a long pause while he tried to think what she was talking about. Eventually, he said, "Oh, yes, thanks. I'd left it on the table after phoning to say Happy New Year to the parents."

"Oh, that's a relief," said Clare with a smile. She suddenly remembered something else that wiped the smile off her face.

"Oh no! I told Brigitte that I would bring along a pudding. I can't possibly make one in this state."

"We must have something in the freezer in the garage left over from Christmas," suggested Nick quickly, apparently relieved to have a change of subject. "I'll go and check." With that, he left the room, leaving Clare to get showered and dressed.

As she stood under the shower, she thought back to last night, trying to remember why she had drunk so much. It was not like her at all. She remembered at one stage Daphne dragging Nick onto the dance floor to shmooz to an old *Four Tops* number. Brigitte had come over with a full bottle of chablis and topped up Clare's glass.

"You are so lucky, cherie, having a husband that will

dance. John will never dance with me."

Clare had felt smug, although it did occur to her that, because so many of the men refused to dance, Nick was very popular on the dance floor. *Oh well, it's all harmless fun,* she'd thought with a shrug.

She stepped out of the shower and slowly got ready for lunch, pulling on a comfortable dress that hid the bumps, along with thick tights and boots. She slapped on some make-up, then joined Nick downstairs. He had raided the fridge, showing off his hunter-gatherer trophies.

"Right, we've got a *Waitrose* stollen or a *Tesco's* cheesecake," he announced. "We also have two dozen mince pies, but I really can't face any more of them."

"Let's take them both," decided Clare, delighted not to be turning up empty-handed. "Are we ready for the off?"

"Yep. Let's go! Round two!" And with that, they set off for John and Brigitte's.

2

John and Brigitte's

The large group of friends was sitting around John and Brigitte's kitchen table, waiting for lunch and dealing with their hangovers with a range of cures. The traditional drinks on New Year's Day were buck's fizz and Bloody Marys, and for the more fragile there was a choice of soft drinks, water, tea, and coffee. The children had again drifted off to the TV room to slump in sofas after their unusually late night. The adults sat around the kitchen table chatting.

After a couple of strong Bloody Marys, John was beginning to feel more human. He checked that Brigitte was out of earshot, then turned and whispered to Daphne: "Come and give me a hand, darling. I need help to bring the wine up from the cellar."

He then said in a louder voice to his wife, Brigitte, "Just off to get the wine, dear. Anyone give me a hand?"

"Oh, go on then," said Daphne, faux-reluctantly, as she traipsed after him down to the sizeable cellar of the large Victorian house. John was a wine buff who loved taking his male friends there to show off his vintage French wines. He was even fonder of taking female friends down there for some slap and tickle.

Once they had negotiated the narrow steps, John pulled Daphne into a clinch. "Come and give Jonny a big kiss, you gorgeous temptress," he murmured into her auburn hair, pulling her into a bear hug. Daphne was only too happy to oblige. Unlike some of her more repressed friends, she saw life as one big joke, and what could be more innocent than a friendly snog? After a kiss and a quick grope she broke free.

"Come on, back upstairs before we're missed," she ordered with a grin, and with that they carried two bottles of claret each back upstairs to put on the table. They had not been gone long enough for suspicions to be raised. Daphne gave her warmest smile to her husband, Marcus, as she sat back down next to him, and John started telling him about the vintage of the wine.

Clare was sitting next to Nick, gazing around the kitchen, staggered as always by the size of the room and the quality of the fittings. Brigitte had had the kitchen added onto her already sizeable house not long ago. It had a double-height roof that rose to an airy, vaulted ceiling, adding to the sense of space. Clare had seen more modest kitchens on the *Food Channel* belonging to TV chefs! It was over ten metres long, with a large cream range, and the long pine table could easily – and often did – seat twenty.

As usual, Clare was imagining how she would redecorate the place if it belonged to her, although it was so tasteful there was little to be done to improve it. With its cream tones, and contrasting touches of burnt umber and faded olive, it was warm and inviting, and one of Clare's favourite places to spend time. Her eyes returned to her friends, where John was holding forth, standing with his hand on the back of a chair to help his balance.

"Thank God that's over with for another year," he declared. "New Year's bloody-Eve! The usual anti-climax…"

"Well, thanks very much!" laughed Daphne, whose wine and champagne John had been happily quaffing the previous evening.

"Oh, Daph, you know I don't mean anything personal," he said, totally unabashed at any offence he might have given. He risked losing his balance by leaning over and giving her a hug, all in the name of making up for any offence caused.

"It's just that it's the one night of the year when we all *have* to be party animals and have fun. It's like enforced entertainment."

"Actually, *you* made a pretty good job of not doing either of those things," snapped Brigitte.

Her usual cheery nature was being strained by her raging hangover, as was her speech. She was only a moderate drinker, so New Year's Day was turning into a tiring day as she'd overdone it the night before. At five foot nothing, there was nowhere for the booze to go. Last night had been a rare evening of over-indulgence. This morning she had tried the buck's fizz before deciding it was not helping her recovery. She moved on to fizzy water and painkillers, and the tablets were just beginning to have some effect.

She was right in what she had said; John had spent most of the evening propping up the bar, happy to discuss sport with any of the men, but that was about the extent of his conversation. He had paid no attention to Brigitte, and refused to dance with her when she had attempted to drag him onto the dance floor. In fact, now she thought about it, she had the vague recollection of dancing alone at some point in the early hours to *The Rolling Stones.*

John ignored Brigitte's comment, and also ignored the fact that she was preparing food for everyone there. He carried on chatting to those seated around him, as Brigitte leant down and started to drag dishes out of the *Aga*, placing them gingerly on the granite central island, while trying to keep the noise down.

"Here, let me help you with those," said Clare, who knew that her friend was suffering as well.

Clare and her sister Lisa stood up to help. The two Taylor sisters were very different in both temperament and looks.

Clare was of average height with mousy hair that she usually pulled back into a scrappy bun or ponytail to keep out of the way. Lisa, by contrast, was tall and willowy, and always made sure she looked immaculate before she set foot outside of her front door. Her hair was not much darker than Clare's, but by the time the hairdresser finished with it every six weeks, it was transformed into several shades of chestnut. Lisa was vigilant with her diet, and weighed herself every other day to ensure that she kept to the size ten she had been since she was eighteen, despite having had two children. Their hair styles gave an indication of their personalities – Clare was as laid back as her casual pony tail, while Lisa was as uptight as her immaculate up-do.

"Come on, everyone, 'elp yourselves," croaked Brigitte, unable to speak normally.

Conversations were interrupted as people started to tuck into the beef casserole, dauphinoise potatoes, and roast vegetables that Brigitte appeared to have produced effortlessly from nowhere, but had actually spent several hours preparing the previous afternoon.

The food began to take effect and soak up some of the excess alcohol that was still floating around inside the more unfortunate bodies around the table. John became the perfect host, and now felt sufficiently revived to move around the table offering the heavy claret to wash down the beef.

The main course was followed by a variety of chilled homemade puddings, helping to raise sugar levels. Clare's shop-bought offerings remained in the fridge. As the puddings were cleared away, and replaced by a vast cheese board, the group picked up conversations again, and the decibel level increased.

Brigitte started to tell her neighbours about her plans for the coming summer. She had spent her childhood in the south of France with her French mother and English father in a small village just outside Nice. She and John planned to drive down, with their son Josh, to visit Brigitte's parents for the summer, as they did most years. People started discussing their own holiday plans.

Clare hadn't really thought about summer holidays yet, other than to have a brief conversation with Nick. They'd agreed that this year they would stay in the UK. Over the years, they had taken holidays on the Continent, but Clare didn't want to deal with the hassle of airports this year. Plus, with all the negative news about the economy, she was worried that if they booked something expensive they might not be able to afford it when the time came. *And there's all that uncertainty in the news about the exchange rate…* she thought, when Brigitte interrupted her.

"What are you doing this summer? Will you stay with Nick's parents again in Spain?" Brigitte asked.

"No thanks!" Clare exclaimed with a grimace.

Five years previously, Nick's parents had sold the large family home and bought a tiny flat ten kilometres inland from Benidorm. With the remaining capital, the retirees had purchased a small place in Abingdon that Nick could keep an eye on while his parents were abroad. When her in-laws had started talking about their plans to buy a home overseas, Clare had been excited at the thought of having the chance to holiday cheaply with Nick's parents in Spain. But the reality had been disappointing. The Spanish flat had been too small to take Clare and Nick, plus their three children. So, on their first and only visit to see the elderly sun-seekers, the family had flown out with a budget airline to nearby Benidorm, booking into a small hotel. They had found the resort to be full of cheap and tacky hotels, sports bars, and restaurants, with signs along the main streets advertising 'Full English Breakfast' and 'Fish 'n' Chips'. After the first day, Nick had turned to Clare and quipped, "I'm not a celebrity – but *please* get me out of here!"

"How do some of these people manage to complete their passport applications?" he had asked Clare one day on the beach, after a fight broke out between two families over sunbeds.

Thank goodness they had only booked for a week and not a fortnight. Since that holiday from hell, they had made their excuses, and only saw Nick's parents when they made their regular visits back to their Abingdon flat.

Lisa overheard summer holidays being discussed, and started bickering with her husband Phil about what they might do for their annual break. Lisa was insisting that they fly to the States, as their girls would love to visit *Disneyland*.

Phil was a self-employed musician and he was pointing out – not for the first time – that he needed to stay in the UK during the summer months in case some work came his way. As he was a session musician he was often called on at short notice to support other musicians, or to work as part of an orchestra. As a compromise to the States, Lisa was suggesting *Disneyland Paris*, but was becoming frustrated with Phil's intransigence to taking the train.

"The whole point of *Eurostar* is for times like this, isn't it?" she demanded. "Look how fast and convenient it is."

"I absolutely agree," he replied, "but what about the cost of last minute fares if I need to come home at short notice?" The more reasonable he was, the more exasperated Lisa became.

"Oh, honestly," she huffed. "You and your precious music."

Clare had been listening to the pair of them quarrelling, when a thought suddenly hit her; her sister Lisa was suffering from status anxiety! How had she never noticed before? Lisa had never shown any interest in visiting the USA before. But Clare remembered a mutual friend mentioning that they were going there next summer, so now Lisa wanted to go as well.

Clare started to mentally itemise the aspects of Lisa's life that she complained about; her house for a start. Lisa was always moaning that she wanted a kitchen like

Brigitte's. Not only could she and Phil not afford it, but there'd be no room in their garden to build one! And she was always saying how much she hated her job working as a medical secretary in the *NHS*. It was also a sore point, in that it was a constant reminder of how she wanted private healthcare, like most of her friends. *She complains about her* Golf*, but it's in better condition than my old* Micra*,* thought Clare. Lisa hankered after an *Audi TT*, despite the fact that her children wouldn't be able to fit in it. But then... Daphne drove one!

Clare continued compiling her list as the others chatted, totally immersed in her thoughts. The next item was Phil's job, which – despite Lisa's complaints - paid for everything other that the private school fees for their two girls. Phil hadn't wanted to send them, as there were excellent state schools in the area, but Lisa had been adamant. It was her salary that paid the school.

Finally, Clare thought of how Lisa fought with Phil every year about whether they could go abroad or not for their summer holidays. Much to Lisa's disgust, it was usually not. Weekend breaks did not count as proper holidays in Lisa's eyes, even if they were to exotic locations. Their last break had been to Istanbul, and Lisa had loved the city. But that was conveniently forgotten in the current debate.

Clare re-joined the conversation, only to find that Lisa and Phil were still disagreeing about holidays. She cut across their spat.

"Hey, why don't we have a group holiday again? Like Blakeney, but without the rain!"

They all laughed at this, remembering the May half term three years ago where six families had hired six cottages along the High Street in Blakeney, a quaint village on the north Norfolk coast. After four days of horizontal rain, Sam, Clare, and Lisa's brother, who had been staying with Clare, had given up on the holiday and driven back to London. Sam had no children, so he had the freedom to do this. The others didn't like to separate their children from their friends, so they stuck the week out. Clare had not been impressed.

"For goodness' sake, Sam, we're Welsh. We're used to a bit of rain! Have you gone soft now that you're living in the south-east?"

"A bit of rain, yes, but this is a monsoon." With that he had packed his bags and returned to London.

By good luck, Clare had booked a little cottage with a range and an open fire. Her memories were of lazy afternoons spent baking cakes with her older daughter, Sally, in a kitchen nicer than her own at home. Meanwhile, Nick had sat in front of the open log fire reading. Pepper, their cocker spaniel, sat at his feet enjoying the warmth of the fire on his woolly coat. Toby and Holly, their two younger children, were young enough not to care about the weather, and had spent most of their time in the games room in another house hired by one of the other families.

Nick looked over from where he was sitting at the far end of the table, and raised an eyebrow at Clare's unexpected proposal. His expression conveyed both disapproval and surprise in equal measure. Nick and Clare would usually discuss their holiday plans together before inviting friends along. Clare looked forward to their summer break with the children and the two of them usually spent hours planning where to go, and what to do when they got there. Clare caught his look, but ignored it. *Oops too late now. Must be the wine,* she thought.

Sam, who'd been quietly listening to his sisters, groaned in mock horror at the mention of Blakeney. "No, thanks. Very kind of you, I'm sure, but we're heading for the sun this year. Gabby and I are planning something slightly more exotic this summer."

As Sam spoke, he turned and gave a soppy smile to his girlfriend. *Ah yes, young love*, thought Clare. Well, not so young, but in its early stages, certainly. In the eighteen months that they had been together, Sam and Gabby had become very much an item.

Sam was thirty-five and worked in the city, which is where he'd met Gabby. She worked for a merchant bank as a P.A. She always turned up elegantly dressed whatever the occasion, with glamorous hair and make-up. In fact, with her high cheek bones, she could be mistaken for a model, although she didn't have the rake-like figure required for the catwalk. She was slim, tanned, and blonde. Clare's only complaint with Gabby was that she was a teeny bit dull, but hey, if Sam loved her that was all that mattered. Gabby, likewise, seemed very smitten with him. Clare was slightly envious of her glamour, not that she would ever admit to it out loud.

As his older sister, Clare couldn't help but be pleased that her brother had found a loving partner. Gabby had not been on the scene at the time of the Blakeney holiday, so the others took great delight in describing the horrors of a deluged Norfolk coast, wildly exaggerating the extent of the rain. By the time they had finished it sounded more like a monsoon!

"Oh goodness, it does sound fun having everyone together for a holiday," she gushed. *How like her to totally ignore all the tales of driving rain spoiling every excursion*, thought Clare.

Gabby turned to Sam. "Couldn't we squeeze in another weenie holiday this year?" she pleaded. As they were still DINKies – double income, no kids – the issue of budgeting wasn't high on either of their agendas.

"We'll see, darling," replied Sam. "Maybe a long weekend. One condition, though… *anywhere* but Blakeney!"

The rest of the afternoon was spent throwing options onto the table, discussing them, then discounting them for various reasons. At the end of two hours they had run through all the obvious holiday destinations. Lisa liked to be organised, so she started to compile a list:

Possible summer holiday locations
Norfolk – never again!
Scotland – too many midges
Ireland – too far for Phil
Devon – too much traffic
Cornwall – we've all done Rock and Padstow
Cotswolds – too close to home
Isle of Wight – too quiet
Yorkshire – too cold
Lake District – too wet
Wales – too far to drive

It was at this point that Sam disagreed with his sister, pointing out that although West Wales and North Wales were indeed hours away, South Wales was only three hours down the M4 motorway. Clare leapt in to add her support.

"Yes, look how often it's done by Gavin!" She was referring to *Gavin and Stacey*, the popular TV comedy.

"Please don't suggest that we go to Barry Island," guffawed John, still enjoying his claret.

Much more of that wine, thought Brigitte, *and you'll be the same size as Smithie.*

Lisa gave John one of the looks that she normally saved for Phil and the children when she was trying to get them to do her bidding, and turned to Brigitte.

"Brigitte, have you got a map so we can show this cretin exactly what he is missing out on by ignoring God's own country!"

Lisa was not to be swayed from her mission to educate the others. General groaning around the table followed Lisa's request. No Welsh person in England was allowed to sing the praises of Wales without having the piss taken out of them.

"Anyway," one of the group pointed out, "isn't New Zealand God's own country?"

Duncan, the only Scot at the table, corrected them all. "Och, you're an ignorant lot south of the border. It's

Scotland that owns that honour."

"Lucky we haven't got an Irishman here, otherwise no doubt he'd be telling us that Ireland deserves the title," commented Phil, highly amused.

The English at the table laughed easily, as they considered their neighbouring countries to be merely an off-shoot of England anyway. This time it was Phil who received the laser stare from his wife, but he was so used to it he happily ignored her. The Taylor family, comprising Clare, Sam, and Lisa, started to get into the swing of extolling the virtues of all things Welsh. Sam even started to hum *Land of my Fathers* but hadn't quite burst into song when Brigitte returned with a UK road atlas.

"Christ, put three Welsh people together and they start a choir!" laughed John.

Sam ignored the comment and found the right page. He laid the atlas open in the middle of the table. He took centre stage and pointed out the Gower peninsular on the south coast of Wales.

"You don't need to drive as far as the west coast. The Gower is amazing. It's an Area of Outstanding Natural Beauty, has one of the best surfing beaches in the UK, great shops in the little town of Mumbles… some nice castles… um… blue flag beaches that win international awards for their natural beauty… what more could you want?"

Lisa joined in with, "Look. You take the M4 all the way there. It's not like West Wales where the motorway stops at Carmarthen, and then you find yourself behind a caravan for the next two hours before you hit the coast."

John leant over to refill his glass, and in the process knocked it all over the atlas.

"Oopsie!" he slurred, giving a lopsided smile and making no move to staunch the spreading red stain that was in danger of spilling onto the floor.

As Clare rushed to fetch some kitchen paper to mop up the pool of wine, she thought his action was deeply symbolic of what he probably thought of Wales. Brigitte, on the other hand, looked at her husband with something less kind in her eyes. *Merde! Drunk again*, she thought, *and it's only four o'clock in the afternoon.*

The conversation moved onto other topics with no firm commitment from anyone to a Welsh holiday. But Clare did make an undertaking that she would enquire about self-catering cottages in Mumbles.

The afternoon continued in a haze of forgotten conversations. As the sun set through the large French windows, parents swept up their children and headed home. The Christmas and New Year holidays were nearly over.

3

The Clothes Horse

It was Monday morning of the following week, and life had returned to its usual routines. Children had started back at school, and adults were back in their hamster wheels of choice.

Clare was in Brigitte's shop, *The Clothes Horse*, marking down clothes for their January sale. The shop sold the sort of stylish, individual brands that could be found in the classier department stores, but not the high street chains.

The town of Abingdon was situated on the banks of the Thames, south of Oxford. Along the towpath could be found interesting historic buildings, such as St Helen's Church, the Abbey ruins, and the Old Gaol. Despite the landmarks' familiarity, Clare still enjoyed walking her dog alongside the meandering river. The shop itself was located just off Abingdon's Market Square, and it fitted in well with the other independent shops in the quaint, narrow, side streets.

As Clare re-priced and moved the clothes from one rail to the next, Brigitte walked in from the tiny back kitchen with two cups of coffee.

"Time for a break!" she ordered, smiling.

Clare was only too happy to sit down for five minutes to chat to her friend.

"How do you think the sale will go?" she asked Brigitte.

"Well, I think it all depends on the weather. A really cold spell would help shift some of these coats and jackets, plus we've still got dozens of scarves and gloves that I thought we would have sold by now. We didn't sell as many as I'd hoped for before Christmas."

Brigitte frowned as she gave a critical look at her stock. Despite her expression, Brigitte, as always, looked glamorous. Her French heritage was only evident by a slight accent, and even that was attractive.

Clare always thought that the fact Brigitte was French was reflected in the chic style of the clothes she stocked, and in the décor of the shop itself. Brigitte had designed the shop interior herself, with her usual good taste and Parisian flair. The floors had been stripped and painted in cream eggshell paint that was wearing to a pleasing, faded finish. The walls were also painted cream and, mounted in strategic places, were large, ornate pewter-framed mirrors. In one corner was a low table, with two upholstered chairs for customers to sprawl in. The fabric for the chairs, and that of the matching changing-room curtains, was a textured, duck-egg blue. The overall impression was one of space and elegance.

Shoppers loved to come in and browse in the relaxing atmosphere. Unlike in anonymous chain stores, regular clients were offered coffee while they browsed. Brigitte would often phone customers when she took delivery of a new season's range from one of their favourite brands.

Clare had started working in the shop four years ago, when her youngest child, Holly, had started at school full-time. She knew that with a good degree in anthropology she could be doing something more demanding, as she had done before the children had been born. She didn't earn much money, but the part-time hours were family-friendly. Brigitte was always accommodating when Clare needed time off, and the work was stress free.

Several of Brigitte's friends worked part-time at the shop, and were available to provide cover during busy times and holidays, so finding occasional staff was never a problem. For Brigitte's friends did not need the income, working in *The Clothes Horse* felt more like a social outing than a job. Brigitte was a good friend, and a relaxed boss, so working in the shop didn't feel like work for Clare. What did they say? *Find a job you love and you'll never have to work again.* Nick was not so approving, but then he had always been dismissive of her degree ever since they'd met at university.

"Honestly, the science of humanity! How's that going to get you a job?" he had commented scornfully when he was told the degree Clare was studying for. In fact, she had left university and walked straight into a well-paid job, which shut him up. She could understand his point of view, of course, as he had been training to be an accountant - and accountancy was nothing, if not practical. Well, she was being practical now by not putting undue pressure on the family. Holding down a challenging job at the same time as raising three children was not for Clare.

No sooner had Clare and Brigitte finished their coffee, than the brass bell over the door clanged as a customer breezed inside out of the cold, bringing a blast of icy air with her.

Jenny was a regular and spent a significant portion of her clothing budget in *The Clothes Horse.*

"Morning, Ladies," she boomed, standing centre stage. "When does the sale start?"

"Not until tomorrow, officially," said Brigitte, "but if you see something that you fancy you can have it at the reduced price. We haven't finished re-tagging all the items yet – too busy drinking coffee! Can I get you one?" She heading for the tiny kitchen.

"Ooh, that would be lovely," said Jenny. "I'm frozen! I really fancy a warm jacket with a hood to keep out the cold. Have you heard? There's snow forecast."

Brigitte caught Clare's eye and smiled. *Good! That should help shift some stock.*

"Oh no! Will that be a problem for you, living out of town?'" Clare asked. Jenny lived in the picturesque little village of Dry Sandford, about four miles west of Abingdon.

"Not at all, I'll be fine," replied Jenny breezily, pointing through the window to where her massive four-by-four was parked. Other vehicles could just about pass it on the narrow road, if they slowed right down. "That beast can get through anything, and it's not as if there are any hills between here and home."

Jenny carried on chatting as she tried on most of the jackets and coats in her size – whether they fitted or not. She had no intention of trying on larger sizes, despite the fact that they might be more comfortable. She eventually settled on a thick grey wool jacket that Clare had secretly had her eye on.

Oh well, Clare thought, *think of the money I'll save*. She certainly didn't need another jacket. It would just have been a smart addition to her wardrobe.

Clare folded the jacket, lining it with tissue paper before placing it in one of the co-ordinated blue and silver bags that customers liked to swing as they sauntered out of the shop. They could show off to other shoppers that they had made a purchase in the exclusive boutique.

As Jenny finished her coffee and was paying, she mentioned a mutual friend of theirs who had left her husband over the Christmas holiday.

"Did you hear about Felix and Lara? He's been playing the field with a woman in his office, and Lara got to hear about it. Poor bitch!"

Gossip while working was a guilty pleasure of Clare's. Customers liked to chat as they shopped, so she often heard juicy snippets of news. This time, however, Clare was not pleased to hear the latest comings and goings. Lara had apparently discovered on Christmas Eve that her husband, Felix, was having an affair, so she had taken their children and gone back to her parents. He was in the process of negotiating an armistice, and trying to get her and the children back home.

After Jenny left, Clare carried on marking price tickets, but she was preoccupied. Anybody passing the shop window would have seen her sitting in the middle of the shop, staring into space, and surrounded by piles of muted-coloured scarves and gloves.

What would life be like for that poor woman now? And why had it all come out during the Christmas holiday? Had it been one of those scenarios that she read about in magazines and newspapers at this time of year? The ones that warned of the increased stresses and strains of families confined together for extended periods of time? What had John called it on New Year's Day… enforced enjoyment?

Brigitte's voice broke into her thoughts.

"Ah, so sad about Lara and Felix. These English men are so stupid to get caught."

"What do you mean?" asked Clare, surprised. "Stupid to have an affair, don't you mean?"

"Of course, married men will have affairs, cherie, as will married women. But to let your wife find out and threaten to end the marriage? Pouf! This is financial suicide. And those poor children. Why would you do that? Is it so difficult to be discreet?"

Clare was shocked. She had not realised that Brigitte's views were so different to her own. "You don't mean that John…?" Clare couldn't finish the sentence.

"Not now, of course, but when he was younger… well, who knows? And that is just the way it should be. You are married a long time, no?"

With that question hanging in the air, Brigitte returned to the stock room to her pricing. Clare could not imagine John ever having an affair, but then, she had not known him in his younger days. He'd certainly looked attractive in old family photos she had seen. Clare had played out the Unfaithful Husband scene many times before in her head, as she had a horror of something similar happening to her. Not that she had any reason to worry, but, even so… On the rare occasions that she and

Nick had argued, or when friends of theirs had split up, like the couple Jenny had just told her about, Clare always felt threatened.

God, how miserable it all was, she thought, putting a black line through a price ticket with rather more pressure than was necessary. The one certainty about this, and all other break-ups, was that the children always suffered.

Clare thought about her relationship with Nick. He was such a good husband and father, thank goodness! Even though he had to work such long hours, he had never strayed. With a heartfelt sigh, and a final selfish thought that she was glad it wasn't her that was dealing with a separation, Clare moved to the windows to consider how she could best display all these gloves and scarves for maximum impact.

Outside, as promised, the snow started to fall.

* * *

In Oxford, meanwhile, Nick, was enjoying being back at work. He had a new secretary who had started with the firm just before Christmas, and he was looking forward to getting to know her. He had been leafing through his diary, wondering how soon he might be able to make use of the company apartment in London. The accountancy firm, for which he was a director, had offices in both Oxford and London.

The Oxford office was in one of the old buildings in the centre of the city. All honey-coloured Cotswold stone, the sort of architecture that the cameramen liked as background shots when filming detective programmes like *Morse* and *Lewis*. The viewers didn't realise that most of the filming had to be done at sunrise so that the crush of tourists was out of shot. When Nick started work very early he sometimes caught the cameras rolling and the stars wandering into view.

Nick much preferred the London office which, in total contrast, was all steel and glass. When no other partners were using the company apartment he would contrive an excuse to work there. He would enjoy himself, living the bachelor lifestyle for a day or two, every couple of months. *Nothing like it for keeping the marriage fresh*, was his considered opinion. Over the years, he had not always been alone on these business trips.

The office was in Bloomsbury, and Nick often walked the streets imagining he was one of the Bloomsbury Set, not that he had ever written anything other than business reports since leaving school.

His last secretary had left the company before Christmas under a cloud. They had had a 'bit of a fling', as he liked to think of it, but she had taken it way too seriously. When he told her he needed to break things off she had made a bit of a fuss. *Silly bitch*, thought Nick, *She had known all along that I was married. What did she expect? After all, I kept a picture of the wife and kids on the desk, just to make it clear where my loyalties lay.*

Unfortunately, the situation had reached the ears of his boss, and he'd been forced to sit through a most embarrassing meeting, where Tom had talked about the need for professional standards in these litigious times. He didn't want the company's name besmirched with a false dismissal claim, blah, blah, blah.

"The bottom line, Nick, is that we have the company name to think of," was Tom's final comment.

The cheeky bastard had suggested that Nick's next secretary not be of the usual tall, blonde, leggy variety. *For Christ's sake*, thought Nick, *can't I have any fun in the office? It's only a bit of innocent flirting, with no strings attached. Nobody gets hurt, after all.*

Nick felt sorry for himself. It wasn't his fault that women threw themselves at him. *I'm just too good looking for my own good.* He was tall and blond, with what Elise, his ill-fated last secretary, had called 'amber eyes.' He rather liked that. Although he hadn't liked it so much when she had told him he had a heart of gold – chicken-shit yellow, and hard!

"You are such a bastard, Nick," had been her final comment as she had stormed out of the office in tears. It wasn't the first time he had heard those words or, he suspected, the last.

Anyway, here he was, a new year and a new secretary. To keep the peace, he had done what Tom advised. Annabelle was short, mousy, and dumpy, and nothing that Tom could complain about. However, she did have the most amazing green eyes, which had been the deciding factor when he gave her the job. *How unusual are green eyes?* He might look it up online. *Now, what would Elise have called those? Not emerald; too dark. Hmm, let's see … could you get green citrine?*

His fingers flicked over the keyboard to do a *Google* search. He watched Annabelle walk across the office and thought that he might suggest she get some blonde highlights. Women liked it when you took an interest in them, and Tom could hardly complain at that, could he? Her weight was going to be more of a problem. He knew women could be a bit touchy about that. The thought of weight made his mind drift from his secretary to his wife. He had made a comment to Clare over Christmas about her eating too many mince pies, and she had given him one of her hurt looks. *Bloody hell, he was only looking after her!* The last thing he wanted was a matron for a wife. All in all, he could congratulate himself on doing quite well with Clare - she was wearing well. He did have to keep reminding her about her weight, but that was for her own good. She wasn't *too* heavy, and she could still wear a bikini without embarrassing him.

He could still remember the first time he had seen her, back in their university days. They had both attended *Sussex University* and met through mutual friends on Brighton beach on a cloudless, hot summer's day. She had been wearing a skimpy bikini, and her curves were shown off to perfection, which is what had attracted Nick to her. She also had the most amazing eyes like Liz Taylor. Not lilac, as hers were said to have been, but bright blue, with heavy eyelashes.

Clare had been flattered by Nick's attention, but he had already been out with two girls she knew, and he had a reputation as a ladies' man. She was reluctant to date him, but he had reassured her early in their relationship, following a particularly successful coupling by telling her, "From now on, Clare, you're the only girl for me. I'm a one-woman guy, and that woman has everything I need to keep me happy." Nick often told her that, normally as she lay naked in his arms.

He had quickly found her to be gentle and easygoing, a perfect foil to his driven, selfish personality. He enjoyed her tender nature. The fact that she trusted him so completely was a novelty that he also enjoyed, and was the clincher in his decision to stick with her.

He'd been studying Business and Accountancy and she was studying Anthropology. He had always made it clear that he thought her degree a waste of time – he had told her that on more than one occasion. Sure enough, once she graduated, she had taken a job as an administrator, never using whatever she'd learnt – not that he ever really knew what that was. It was a well-paid job and, combined with Nick's salary, enabled them to buy their first home on the outskirts of Oxford. He had started his accountancy exams, and they had married in their late twenties.

Once their first child had come along, they moved to a larger house in Abingdon, near to Nick's parents. When they could afford it, they moved again to their present large, detached home. Clare had given up work to be a full-time mother, at least until the children started school.

And now she's wasting her time working in that stupid clothes shop, he thought to himself, back to the present with a frown. Nick tutted out loud, then stood up to pick up a file from the other desk. He turned his attention, at last, to his work.

4

Lisa & Phil

"Phil, I distinctly remember telling you that you had a school date tonight." Lisa was spitting feathers.

Phil, her husband, had just told her that he wouldn't be able to attend Ellen's parents' evening. He looked up from his breakfast muesli.

"Sorry, hon, but a gig has come up." He shrugged, as if to say that was the end of the matter.

"But I've got my book club meeting this evening!"

"What can I say? Do you want me to cancel? Really?" He gave her a look to suggest that she was being unreasonable.

Their youngest daughter, Ellen, was twelve, and not doing as well at her studies as her sister Sophie, who was fourteen and starting her GCSEs. Lisa didn't want to turn up for bad news about Ellen. *Damn it*, she thought, *I'm going to have to go and face the music*. And she would miss her book club meeting, which was more of a social event than a cultural gathering.

The girls' school was a former manor house in its own grounds, on the outskirts of Oxford. When Sophie had first started there Lisa had felt a rush of excitement every morning when she had driven through the gates and up the long tree-lined drive. She was pleased to be part of this exclusive enclave. As the bills had dropped on the mat each term, the novelty had quickly worn off, especially now that she was paying for both girls.

"The trouble with Ellen is that she's just like you – too laid back!" Lisa complained to Phil.

He smiled at that, rather liking the fact that his lovely

little girl was being compared to him. Her hair was always in her eyes and her socks always at half mast, and these traits were indicative of her relaxed manner. Ellen was unconcerned by such superficial trivialities as dressing smartly. All she cared about was music. Her elder sister Sophie was, by contrast, always in the top ten per cent in her class, so Lisa expected the same performance from Ellen.

Sophie was more like her mother. She was always immaculate, even for school, and spent more money on hair and beauty products than the rest of the family put together.

Lisa and Phil were an unlikely couple. People meeting them together for the first time were usually surprised at the pairing. Lisa was quite uptight, while Phil was relaxed and easy-going. What was that saying about opposites attracting? They were also opposite in style; unless Phil was wearing a black tie ensemble for a concert, he lived in worn cargo pants and rugby shirts, despite Lisa's efforts to smarten him up.

When Lisa had met Phil fifteen years earlier, she had loved the fact that he was a musician. She had thought it very romantic that he travelled around with his job and did not do the usual, boring nine-to-five like everyone else she had ever met. He looked like her ideal image of a musician, with long wavy hair and formal suits when he performed. He'd looked like the guys she saw on the front of classical music magazines.

When they'd started dating, he would sit at his piano serenading her with ballads, and occasionally compose a song dedicated to her. On top of that, as he had become more established, he took her to concerts when he was performing. Lisa used to love to name-drop the household names of celebs she had seen, and sometimes met. *God, it seems like a lifetime ago!*

As the years had gone by, their two girls had arrived to cramp her style. The novelty of music had paled, and nowadays she took more interest in how much money Phil's music was making, rather than how it sounded. She glanced at him now. *Honestly, my friends' dogs are better groomed than you are.*

She was still glowering at the back of his head as he made to leave the room. As he walked out, Sophie entered the room, making excellent use of her education by circumnavigating the furniture while texting.

"Mum, have you got that cheque for me for school tomorrow?" she asked, still texting. "Mr Jeffs wants the final instalment for the ski trip."

Having delivered her message she didn't wait for a reply but turned on her heels and traipsed out, without once having looked up from her phone. Lisa now glared at Sophie's back, before angrily scribbling out the cheque.

She dragged her thoughts back to the present problem. When Ellen started to fall behind in her work, Lisa had taken immediate action with additional tutoring. Phil, on the other hand, hadn't been concerned. Ellen was musical like him; she played the Spanish guitar confidently. Although, she struggled to pass the music exams to give her those all-important grades for her CV. This was something that both the school and Lisa felt were more important than whether she had natural ability, or even enjoyed playing.

Phil thought otherwise. As a professional musician, he recognised Ellen's keen ear for music, and encouraged her to pick up her guitar, sometimes to accompany him on the keyboard. He thought that it was far more important for her to enjoy playing than be pushed harder and harder to get good grades, but he knew that he was in the minority on this topic.

Lisa was not prepared to make excuses for Ellen's moderate, (read unsatisfactory), progress. Lisa had booked a private dyslexia consultation, and was hopeful that Ellen would pass (or was that fail?) the test. Two of Ellen's friends were dyslexic and they were given extra time to complete their exams. Lisa was sure that if Ellen could have the same it would make the difference to her getting back to the top half of her class.

Another factor weighing heavily on Lisa's mind was her desire for the girls to weekly board. Boarders at the school did all their homework under the watchful supervision of teaching staff. *That must surely improve the quality of their grades*, thought Lisa. More to the point, it would save her having to keep track of all their assignments and projects, which was tedious in the extreme. Obviously, she dipped in and helped where she could, but even so, there seemed to be a continuous list of deadlines to meet. She had broached the matter of boarding with Phil, but he'd just shrugged and walked off. Their bank balance spoke for itself. He didn't even bother to say.

And that's another thing, thought Lisa crossly. *When are we sorting out the kitchen?* She had been nagging Phil for months to consider a small extension, or knocking into another room, but he wasn't interested. *Well, he should try spending more time cooking here. Then he might realise how pokey it is!* Spending New Year's Day in Brigitte's designer kitchen had reminded her, yet again, of how she had to suffer with her galley kitchen. Their house was a typical Victorian semi, in a quiet Abingdon road that most people would be delighted to live in, but Lisa was finding it too cramped now that the children were growing. *And why do there have to be so many musical instruments everywhere?*

Lisa felt that life was treating her unfairly, and that she was somehow *due* a more lavish lifestyle than she had at present. The fact that most of her salary went on school fees really rankled with her. *Honestly, Clare can only afford the luxury of her little part-time job because she's happy to pack her kids off to the local comp without a care in the world about their future prospects. Really, you would think that Nick would want them to have a better education.*

True, Sally and Toby, Clare's two elder children,

appeared to be thriving, and did have some very nice friends. But, Lisa knew that both her girls needed that extra boost than only private education could provide.

She had raised the subject of weekly boarding when she made one of her rare phone calls to her mother in Wales. She hoped her mother might have a little nest-egg hidden away that might be put towards a worthwhile cause. Her mother soon put her straight. "Boarding?" Enid had exclaimed loudly on the other end of the phone. "Why on earth would you want the girls to board? The school's only ten miles away, for heaven's sake!"

"Twelve, actually," corrected Lisa, "and when you're making that journey twice a day, sometimes more, it can take up most of the day. Don't forget that I do also work."

She omitted to mention that she chose to take the children herself rather than share some of the journeys with other mothers. Well, she couldn't trust someone else to always being on time for her precious girls. Phil helped occasionally, when he was home, but she also distrusted his memory, and tonight was a case in point. She followed Phil into the music room to continue to berate him.

"What is so important this evening that you can't go to the school?" she demanded. He looked at her in disbelief, feigning an open-mouthed stare.

"Sweetheart, it's work, otherwise of course I would take Ellen. It's what pays the bills, remember?" The mention of earning money usually sweetened Lisa's mood.

"I sometimes wonder whether it's worth being married to you," Lisa continued, as if Phil hadn't spoken. "You're never around to help me, and when you are here, you put your headphones on, so I can't even talk to you."

"I put my headphones on so that you can't hear the keyboard when I'm playing, as requested by you. You complain about the din, as you call it, when I don't plug them in." He looked up and smiled at her with infinite patience. "Which is it you want?"

Ooh, he was so reasonable. Lisa didn't bother to

answer. She wanted to hit him, just for being so… self-satisfied. Of course she wanted him to work, but just not tonight, of all nights. Now, she would have to turn up to face lectures from Ellen's teachers.

She and Phil rubbed along together well enough but, after fifteen years, the passion had certainly dimmed, and Lisa sometimes wondered what it would be like to start again with someone else. What was that saying? 'Better dead than divorced.' It made sense to her. If, say, he died. Maybe in a car crash - quick and without any pain, obviously. She and the girls would grieve, but their lives would move on. She was sure she could find a replacement, after a suitable period of mourning, naturally.

Divorce, on the other hand, was a dreadful limbo-land of court cases and custody battles, if you both still wanted to see the kids. Phil would still be around for the girls' weddings (white, church, of course) and there would be all those arguments over who would give the girls away, and if the new wife should attend the ceremony. *God forbid – he might even have a new family*!

The thought of dealing with Phil's imaginary new family made Lisa feel so upset that she grudgingly had to admit that she might, after all, be better off with him, than without him. *Just!*

She shouted for the girls to get into the car for school and returned to Phil with a final sally.

"Right, tomorrow we need to go through our diaries to check what work you have booked. I don't want you working through our summer holiday. Think of the girls."

With that closing piece of emotional blackmail, she felt she had made her point, and stalked out of the room, leaving Phil to his keyboard.

5

London Calling

It was a fine evening in early April, and Nick was spending two nights in Canary Wharf. He was sitting on the balcony of the company apartment looking out over the Thames, and congratulating himself yet again on his good fortune. He had always enjoyed visiting London in the days before the children had come along, and was delighted when he landed a job which enabled him to work regularly in the city. He enjoyed all the benefits of family life in the country, and could still pursue what he liked to think of as a single lifestyle when working in London. He'd work in the Bloomsbury office during the day, before travelling east to the apartment.

He glanced around to see if anything had changed since his last visit two months ago, but all seemed in place. The company had purchased the flat off-plan as an investment several years ago. It had proved to be a financial success, as well as providing a base for staff who needed to do business. The company also put up foreign clients in the apartment, so there was a concierge service. This meant that whenever Nick arrived there was clean linen on the bed, and fresh towels in the bathroom. If he had a female 'companion' he could order flowers and champagne on his company account – the concierge was the soul of discretion.

The décor in the flat was sterile and modern, unlike his home in Abingdon that was chintzy and homely. It had been styled in muted shades of cream and stone that were so tasteful they wouldn't look out of place in a *Kelly Hoppen* magazine spread. Nothing here was recycled, upcycled, vintage, or any other variant of second hand. Kirsti Allsopp would not have approved.

The lounge had a mink-coloured suede suite, a massive TV, and a small oval glass dining table with matching suede dining chairs. Practicality was not an issue here. The kitchen was compact, but contained all the essentials above and below its glistening granite counters: fridge, in-built oven, microwave, juicer, and coffee maker. Not that Nick had ever cooked there. There were two bedrooms, both en-suite, and again all in neutral colours.

The best feature of the apartment was the view, which gave the place its wow-factor. One entire wall of the lounge was glass, comprising of sliding doors leading out to a large balcony. It caught the afternoon and early evening sun, and was wide enough to hold seats and a small table. It also had a roof provided by the balcony above, meaning that you could sit out in wet weather – a boon in the U.K. Nick often marvelled at British architecture that was designed by people apparently oblivious to the amount of rainfall typical in summer. He was sitting out there now in the evening sun, grateful for the weak rays disappearing over the buildings on the other side of the river. *This block must have been designed by an architect on a day when he got soaked in a summer downpour. That had focused his mind on keeping dry outdoors. And hooray for that.*

Nick poured champagne into a glass and took stock. Life was good, he decided. Yes, work was hard graft, but it paid for a quality lifestyle and he was on track to retire at sixty. That thought kept him going on many a dull Monday morning. He had a great house and a fantastic wife. Clare ran the home like clockwork, and didn't interfere with his side of things at all – his job and the household finances. She let him get on with his life without giving him the third degree like some women he knew did with their husbands. And the kids were great. The girls were real poppets. Sal was very like her mum, calm and practical, while Holly had a mix of them both, still quite a tomboy. *Yeah,* he concluded, *great kids and a great wife.*

Toby was taking to sport just like his old man, and turning out for the school touch-rugby team. He was a good cricketer too, and had joined the junior section of the local cricket club. *It keeps him off those damned computer games if nothing else. You never know; with luck he could be the next Freddie Flintoff, and I'll be able to watch him play at* Lords *and* The Oval. *He'd surely be able to get tickets for family?*

He loved the Thames, both here in the built-up Docklands, and at home in Oxfordshire where it seemed like another river, much smaller and slower. *Just like the difference between the city of London and the town of Abingdon,* he thought with a smile. The lights were beginning to twinkle in the night sky and he could see the dome of the *O2 Arena* to the south.

Clare had only stayed at the apartment the one time, using the children and work commitments as her excuse to not visit more often. She found London too busy, noisy, and dirty. To be honestthat suited Nick fine. He had taken her to see Katherine Jenkins sing at the *O2* on that one and only visit. He had enjoyed the evening, not because he liked her singing particularly, but because he had really wanted to see Katherine in the flesh. She was a beautiful woman. He tried to picture her naked, and naturally liked the image that his mind conjured up. *Hadn't she been recently linked to Beckham? The fact that she bothered to deny it means it must be true. I wouldn't mind giving her one. He was one lucky boythat David. Who had it been before that? Rebecca Loos, his assistant? She had ended up on a reality TV show doing something very undignified to a pig. So much for fifteen minutes of fame! I'll do without the fame, thanks, and just have the money.*

Nick was just about to drift further into fantasy-land with Katherine, when his current, real-life fantasy drifted out of the bedroom, very much in the flesh. Annabelle, his secretary, walked out to join him on the balcony, dressed only in the skimpy silk negligee that Nick had bought for her earlier that day.

Annabelle and Nick had spent the early evening shopping in *Harrods*. The first time he bedded one of his secretaries – his 'Babes' – he'd take them to *Harrods* and buy them expensive underwear. 'I can imagine you wearing it when we're in the office,' he would murmur seductively, as if from a script.

On other visits to the apartment he would take them to *Harrods* and buy them perfume. 'I'll be able to smell your scent all day. It'll be our little secret.' *God, he was smooth.* They always went for *Chanel No. 5* – the Marilyn Monroe connection – but he had to steer them away from that as it was Clare's favourite. He had bought it for her on their first Christmas together, and every Christmas since. He couldn't bear having that in the office – it would remind him of home.

Annabelle gave a twirl. "What do you think?" she asked coyly.

"Ravishing," he murmured. "Come to Daddy."
He gave her an appreciative smile and held out a glass of champagne for her. Nick couldn't help drawing a quick comparison between her outfit and what Clare usually wore around the bedroom – leggings and baggy tops, often sporting 'cute' cartoon animals on the front. *Honestly, who designed them? Fine for the Bridget Joneses of this world, but not an option for any woman who actually had a man and wanted to keep him interested.* Just thinking about it made him angry. He had been buying Clare sexy underwear for her birthday every year since they were married, but he might as well not bother for all the effort she made to wear it to tantalise him. *If I do stray, she can only blame herself,* he thought with self-righteous pity, slipping his arm around Annabelle's luscious buttocks.

***

Back home in Abingdon, Clare was snuggled up on the sofa watching TV in those self-same pyjamas. They were her favourite ones, with a sheep on the front sewn in a woolly fabric. *So sweet*, she thought. The children were in their rooms, supposedly asleep in bed, and she was curled up with Pepper next to her. *Poor Nick,* she thought, as she fondled Pepper's ears, *having to stay up in that horrible, sterile flat all alone. I know he hates it. He always comes home in a bad mood after he's been working there.*

She sat, watching a TV chef pretend to make cooking a casserole look easy, and decided to try and replicate the dish for tomorrow's evening meal. *That'll cheer him up. What do they say? The way to a man's heart is through his stomach?*

She sent him a text:

Wish you were here. Sleep well. C xx

A text came winging back:

I will. Love you N x

She sighed contentedly, and Pepper echoed the sentiment; he might get to sleep on the bed, with the master away.

6

Easter Barbeque

"Christ, low fat sausages! Whatever next?" complained John. He glanced at the labels, as he opened packets of sausages, and threw them haphazardly onto the large gas barbeque. This way he could give the kids hot dogs as soon as they arrived, and get them out of the way before the decent meat was put on the barbie for the adults.

John's love of food and drink was beginning to show on his waistline and by his florid complexion. Brigitte occasionally tried to steer him away from rich food and alcohol when she felt inclined, but with little success. After a week or two of him stomping around like a bear with a sore head, she would shrug her shoulders with Gallic indifference and return to stocking the fridge with the stilton and paté that he loved. *At least I tried*, she would tell her conscience.

Brigitte had hoped that he was going to keep separate all the various sausage flavours that she'd spent so long choosing, and managed to bite her tongue and not interfere. John enjoyed cooking on a barbie – the only time that he did cook – so she might as well take advantage of his catering skills this afternoon. She returned to the kitchen and started preparing a potato salad, checking her list yet again to make sure that there would be enough food for the crowd that was turning up later. There would be other friends, as well as the usual gang of eight couples, plus a horde of ravenous children, so she had a lot to prepare. She put a pan of potatoes on the hob to boil, and started to make a pasta salad when there was a knock at the door and Clare walked in.

"Hi! I thought you might want to put these somewhere out of the way for later on," she explained, walking to the counter with two large puddings as her contribution to the day's catering.

"Oh, wow!" said Brigitte as she caught sight of the chocolate tortes. "I wish I could make puddings like you."

Clare smiled. "It's a really easy recipe, honestly," she replied, but was pleased by the compliment just the same. They had taken hours to make." She continued, "The weather forecast said no rain, so that's good news. Do you want a hand with anything?"

The two women started chatting about the dishes that were being brought by the others, although they both knew there would be more than enough. Sure enough, when the food was served later, everyone piled their plates high, with plenty left over for seconds - and thirds for those that weren't watching their waistlines.

Clare looked out of the French windows. The garden looked wonderful in the bright afternoon sun. Brigitte and John both loved gardening, and spent hours working on the borders to arrange a display of shrubs and flowers in differing shades and heights to show their flower beds off to their best advantage. John worked from home as an online stock trader, and often took advantage of quiet spells to potter around the garden, improving the flower beds. There were three patios at various points around the landscaped lawns, and today all the sun umbrellas were up, giving a festive air to the floral scene.

The lower half of the large garden was wooded, with a further patio sited under overhanging branches. Seating was available for those who made the effort to stroll through the dappled shade below the tall trees. Brigitte loved the mature rhododendrons that were just coming into flower with white and pink blooms, which contrasted brightly against the variety of shady-green hues of the trees. Between the spinney and the lawns was John's pride and joy – a pond containing expensive koi carp. They were a lot of work to maintain, but he liked to watch them glide through the water. Clare wandered out through the French windows to join the first arrivals, and saw her brother approaching with Gabby.

"This is great," said Sam, gazing admiringly around the grounds.

Clare pointed out the features of interest, trying to remember some of the Latin names of the huge array of summer plants. Groups of people were casually seated at the tables and chairs scattered around the various terraces and patios. Sam hadn't been in John and Brigitte's garden before. In the past he tended to avoid family parties where children would be present, but that was before the arrival of Gabby.

"Gabby and I will have to have everyone around for a house-warming lunch once we get settled in," he announced.

He turned and smiled at Gabby, who today looked like Grace Kelly, dressed in citrus orange Capri pants with a tight white top. White sandals on her feet, with orange tassels, finished the outfit off perfectly.

"No kids, of course, as there won't be the room," he continued casually.

He was totally oblivious to the bombshell he had just dropped. Sam had never entertained more than two people in his life, and didn't understand the delicate politics that was played out by parents everywhere when children were not allowed to social events during the day. Babysitters were often harder to find at lunchtimes, and some parents seemed to think that they should not be separated from their children during the hours of daylight. Clare decided to enlighten him about the reality of parenthood some other time.

With this token contribution made to chat with the ladies, Sam walked over to talk to John about the latest football saga and to check how the lamb chops were doing on the barbeque.

Clare turned to Gabby. "How's the house-hunting going?"

"Well, we've seen something we like in Marylebone, but we haven't exchanged yet, so we're keeping our fingers crossed."

Gabby started to witter on about her new home, describing the flat that they had been to see, and Clare listened, pleased that her brother had chosen such a lovely girl to settle down with. *No wonder she looks so smart if she shops on Marylebone High Street*, Clare thought wistfully, admiring her trousers and fitted top, with co-ordinated wedge sandals and straw handbag. She was even wearing a matching sun hat. Clare never felt comfortable in hats, and always envied those that wore them with no signs of being self-conscious. Although the clothes sold by Brigitte in *The Clothes Horse* were very stylish, they were definitely targeted at the slightly more mature woman; she couldn't imagine Gabby shopping there.

Gabby still dressed like a youngster, and could carry it off, even though she was in her early thirties. *Mind youthat's what not having kids does for your figure,* thought Clare again, aware of her own waistline, which had not returned to its pre-child size since the birth of Holly, her third child. *How did these French mamans manage*, she mused, glancing over at Brigitte. *Did they live on cucumber salads?*

As Gabby chatted, Clare's mind continued to drift from one trivial topic to the next. *I must ask where Gabby has her hair coloured - it's seriously smart.* Clare's hair was natural, and the colour was more like something that *Farrow and Ball* might suggest to put on your kitchen wall than a hair shade from a fashion magazine. Nick had spotted a grey hair the other day, and suggested it might be time for some highlights.

Just then, Toby, Clare's middle child, sprinted up with Josh, Brigitte's only child.

"Mum, can Josh come back with us for a sleep-over? He wants to try out my new computer game and it's

Saturday so there's no school tomorrow."

"Sure, as long as that's okay with Brigitte. Check with her first."

The boys ran off to find Brigitte, leaving Clare to continue listening with half an ear to Gabby prattling on about her soft-furnishing options. She watched Toby run away, and was pleased to note that he was a good head taller than Josh, who was of average height. Toby had the broad shoulders and slim hips of his father, with the same light brown eyes.

Thinking of Nick made her glance around to see what he was up to. She spotted him supporting John with his cooking in the best way that he could think of. This entailed picking the best cuts of meat to eat directly off the barbeque as they became available, and at the same time keeping them both topped up with a decent burgundy. She noticed that he had placed the bottle behind the barbeque, just in case it was accidently picked up by anyone who did not have the good taste to appreciate it.

"Don't want the wives nabbing this one," he had confided to John, indicating the label.

Lisa strolled over to join Clare and Gabby.

"While the family is together, I thought I'd check how far we've got with booking the holiday cottages for the summer, if at all," said Lisa to Clare.

"I've just emailed Mumbles Seaside Cottages to check availability," replied Clare. "I've found two at the top end of the town, right on the promenade. They're old fishermen's cottages – really sweet. I'll drop round tomorrow with the brochure for you to look at."

Clare was about to ask Gabby if she and Sam wanted her to find a property for them, when Daphne glided over hugging a bottle of wine to her chest. She worked in marketing and took lots of trips abroad, which Clare envied madly, although Daphne insisted it was tedious in the extreme. Clare promptly forgot about Mumbles and was about to ask Daphne about her recent trip to Rome, but didn't get the chance.

"Look what I've found," Daphne grinned gleefully, with a glint in her eyes. "One of the chaps opened this and left it to breathe, so I've snaffled it." The bottle was an expensive, vintage Bordeaux. "Come on, drink up, we don't want you mixing your wines."

The husbands in the group had gradually become complicit in an unspoken agreement that their wives did not have the refined palate that the men had to appreciate good wine. With this in mind, they sometimes bought bog-standard bottles of red and white in large amounts for general consumption. However, as the day progressed, expensive bottles would magically appear, to be poured out on male-only rounds. Occasionally one of the ladies would put her glass out for a top-up, unaware of what was going on, and a small measure would be poured out through a tight smile before the bottle swiftly moved on.

Daphne, who was a heavy drinker, had caught the men out on one such occasion, and accused them of treating the women like second-class citizens. They had all denied the accusation, but their actions suggested otherwise.

Since Daphne had pointed out this double-standard, Clare had become quite adept at holding her glass out to be filled when she noticed the 'premier cru' bottles coming out from hiding. However, as she wasn't a heavy drinker her occasional top-ups were not resented. In fact, now that Daphne had made Clare aware of the deceit, she found it rather comical to see how hard the men worked to finesse the art of avoiding giving the good wine to the women, especially to Daphne, who was capable of drinking several bottles without falling over. After the first two bottles, even Clare had to concede that Daphne's palate might not warrant drinking bottles at fifty quid a pop.

Clare and Lisa dutifully finished their drinks and held

out their glasses to be refilled. Daphne filled their glasses. Gabby demurred, as she was enjoying sparkling water. Five minutes later, Daphne's usually urbane husband Marcus approached, with a scowl on his face.

"You haven't appropriated something you shouldn't, have you, darling?" he murmured in Daphne's ear, trying to hide his annoyance in front of the others. Daphne held the bottle behind her back and gave him a wide-eyed look of innocence.

"I've got nothing, sweetheart. I'm just standing here, listening to these girls planning their holidays – something we need to start doing before everything gets booked up. They say it's going to be a scorcher this summer." Marcus ignored her attempt to change the subject.

"What's that you're holding behind your back?" he demanded, still managing to keep his voice pleasant.

"Oh… what… this?" asked Daphne sweetly, holding up the bottle of Bordeaux for Marcus to see. A slow flush of anger crept over Marcus' face.

"That's *my* fucking wine, Daphne," he hissed quietly, all pretence of good manners forgotten. "I brought it especially for John to try, as he's thinking of buying some as an investment. Hand it over!" He managed not to blink, or break eye contact, as he told Daphne this outrageous lie.

"Fine," snapped Daphne. "If John wants a taste, then send him over here and I'll pour him a glass to try. There should be just enough left." With that, she poured herself a second glass. Marcus was furious, but he made one last attempt at trying to sound pleasant in front of the others.

"Okay, just let me take some for John to try, and I'll bring the rest back for you girls." He gave the 'girls' a rictus-grin that did not reach his eyes. Daphne was enjoying his discomfort too much to hand over the bottle, and shook her head.

"I don't think so. If you take it, we'll never see it again."

Marcus tried to retain his show of good humour – at least superficially – but then Daphne started to laugh at his annoyance, and Clare joined in, as she was in on the joke. Gabby looked on, totally mystified. Marcus lost his patience and made a grab for the bottle, but Daphne took a neat side-step, leaving him tottering forward and snatching at fresh air.

Nick spotted the incident from across the lawn and shouted out to him. "Come on, Marcus, you used to tackle better than that when you were playing rugby!"

Those that heard the comment looked over to watch what was happening. Marcus now had an audience. His face turned the shade of purple that develops when you are trying not to create a scene but wishing – so wishing – that you could. He cursed quietly as Daphne held the bottle in front of him as a taunt. He made another grab for it, and as he did so, Daphne lifted it above her head. He sprawled onto his stomach, landing with enough force to make his body judder. General laughter broke out from those watching, apart from Gabby. She knelt beside him to help him up, making him feel even more embarrassed.

"Don't worry, Gabby," shouted Sam. "He's capable of getting up without your help – just!"

More laughter ensued, especially from the male friends when they saw that Marcus had a face like thunder. Marcus was now furious, but Daphne had already drunk enough wine to be totally oblivious.

"Silly sod!" she teased, looking down at him. "Why don't you go and have a drink of that lovely *Jacob's Creek* that's in the kitchen? It's what I was drinking before I found this bottle. I think you'll find it perfectly acceptable." With that parting shot, she turned her back and returned to Lisa, still with the remains of the Bordeaux in her hand.

"Come on, Lisa, let me top you up," said Daphne with a hint of victory in her smile. She made to pour some wine into Lisa's glass just as Phil and Nick approached them to see why their friend was cavorting around. Nick caught Daphne's comment and put his hand over Lisa's glass to prevent Daphne pouring.

"No point, Daphne," said Phil, "I'll get the wine you were drinking earlier. If this is Marcus's wine, Lisa won't have any. She doesn't really appreciate vintage wine." Nick smiled as he made this cutting remark, intending to reduce the impact of the insult.

Lisa turned to her brother-in-law in amazement, too stunned to reply. She glared at him, struggling to retort with something rude, as he gave her what he presumed was a winning smile. *How dare he make that decision for me?* she thought. *Plus, how dare he be so dismissive about my ability to enjoy good wine. Ooh, these men! They're so annoyingly clubby!*

Unfortunately, Phil thought Nick's comment rather funny, and gave a snort of laughter. Lisa turned to glower at Phil, for once too angry to come up with a retort. She linked her arm through Daphne's and walked away, leaving the two of them with Marcus. Marcus had to admit defeat – he knew he would not get the wine back now without making even more of a scene. He consoled himself with the knowledge that he had another two bottles stashed in the boot of his car, so he wandered off to open one. This time he would hold onto it, so that Daphne wouldn't get her hands on it.

Daphne was cock-a-hoop at catching out Marcus. Lisa, on the other hand, was now in a blue funk over what she felt was Phil's undermining of her in front of their friends. So, she didn't speak to him for the rest of the afternoon. They managed to get home and see the children to bed before having an almighty row about how Phil had belittled her in front of all of their friends. Lisa attacked and Phil defended, although his heart wasn't really in it.

"It didn't mean anything, darling," he countered weakly. He couldn't say much else, as he knew he was right, because Lisa actually *didn't* appreciate expensive wines. Lisa eventually brought the argument to a close by heading for the spare bedroom. She was wondering – not for the first time – what couples that didn't have a spare bed did at times such as these.

7

Collecting Cockles

Clare woke to the sound of rain on the windows. *So much for a flaming June*, she thought with a sigh. She had gone to bed with the window open and she could imagine the trees in the orchard showering the water from their leaves onto the lawn below. On days such as these, even the Thames could look dreary and sluggish. She lay under the heavy duvet wondering where to go for her morning walk. She looked at the bedside clock – it was too early to get the children up.

She turned over and stretched. It was lovely having the bed to herself. Poor Nick had to work in London for three days, but as compensation she could have the family cocker spaniel, Pepper, on the bed with her. When Nick was home Pepper wasn't allowed to sleep upstairs, which went against the wishes of the rest of the family. Pepper was a wonderful family pet, following the children around all day, especially if they had any food with them! It was an unspoken secret that he might not be the smartest dog in the world, and would probably never win *Crufts*, even though he did have a pedigree. But they all loved him anyway. When Nick had insisted that he was not allowed upstairs, the children attempted to wear their father down by repeatedly boycotting the embargo, but to no avail. Even Pepper had done his best to support their case when he was brought home as an eight week old puppy, by whining in the kitchen for night after night in an attempt to join his favourite people upstairs, but still without success.

Clare had done her best to intercede on behalf of the

children, but Nick was insistent, and had finally declared, "That bloody animal is not allowed upstairs, and that's final. If I find him up there one more time, he'll feel my boot up his backside!"

The rest of the family reluctantly gave up on the battle. Clare recognised the difference of opinion as one of those situations that called for a compromise, as so often happens in marriages where both sides have to concede occasionally. Clare did not consider when the last time was that Nick had been the one to compromise, which was just as well.

Just another five minutes before my walk, she thought, and pulled the duvet around her. She started to make a mental list of her jobs for the day. It was her day off from *The Clothes Horse*, so she had the day to herself; once she had walked the dog, dropped the children off at their two schools, done the washing and ironing, cooked the evening meal; and booked the cottages for herself and Lisa for their summer holiday on the Gower.

As her mind drifted to thoughts of Wales, she remembered a memory from her childhood - of when she used to go collecting cockles in Burry Port with her grandparents. Burry Port was further down the Carmarthenshire coast than the Gower, and the area had been famous for its cockles when she was a little girl. Gradually, however, many of the cockle beds had drifted towards the Gower, and most of the commercial cockling was now carried out in Penclawdd, on the western Gower coast.

Clare remembered one of the last times she had been cockling as a child with Sam, Lisa, their parents, and grandparents. They had all walked to the old harbour at Burry Port from her grandparent's cottage. Her mother's parents had always lived in the small seaside town and lived only ten minutes' walk from the sea. Granny and Grandad lived in a large, old cottage two roads back from the beach. So, although it was cramped when the family descended, the children had loved staying there as they could walk to the beach.

Standing on the beach on Burry Port sandbanks with the tide out, the Gower looked close enough to walk to, but looks were misleading. The vast sandbanks hid a tapestry of estuaries and pools that swirled and eddied with the tides. Her grandad always used to joke about the view.

"If you can see the Gower,' he would say, 'it's about to rain; if you can't see it, it's already raining." He would then have a little chuckle to himself.

His local knowledge meant that he always knew when the tides made it safe to go out onto the sand. They all had to wait for low tide when the sandbanks were exposed, then wade out in wellies or bare feet, with their parents carrying a large, empty galvanised bucket and garden rakes. When their grandfather thought they might be in the right place, the adults would rake the wet sand for the cockles while the children squished their feet into the sand, revealing mud underneath, which is where the molluscs liked to live. As they twisted their feet, they felt for the rough edges of the cockle shells on their bare skin. They would then scoop up the cockles with delightfully mucky hands.

When Sam got bored of cockling he would make mud pies to throw at the girls, making them shriek and chase after him. Another of his games was to pick up a large crab that might occasionally be found in the rivulets left by the receding sea. He would hold one up and walk towards his sisters, who again felt the need to shriek and run out of the reach of its big claws. *Toby has a lot in common with his Uncle Sam*, thought Clare, not for the first time.

While the children enjoyed themselves without a care in the world, the adults kept a keen eye on the distant water to ensure they called everyone back to safety before they were cut off by the fast incoming tides. The tides in the Bristol Channel were well-known locally for their potential danger as they produced treacherous undercurrents. The tidal range between high and low tides was the second deepest in the world, and so when they turned, they had stronger currents than around much of the British coastline. In fact, their grandad had lost two of his friends to these waters as a boy.

Due to these strong undercurrents, it was not uncommon for drownings to occur. The RAF's search and rescue helicopter was a common sight, circling over the beaches along the Carmarthenshire coastline. While the children played on the beaches without a care, their parents would look up at the helicopters and think of the poor swimmer who might have been carried out by the tides. The children, on the other hand, thought that it was fantastically exciting to have the helicopters circling low overhead, and would shout and wave at the pilot as he and his crew scanned the water for a body.

On those long-ago cockling days, the children would search for cockles until the bucket was about half-full, then the family would all head back above the high water mark, pausing to wash all the mud and sand from their feet in the shallows, and to put their shoes back on. Then it was back to Granny's to clean the cockles.

When they got home, the first task was to put the bucket of shells in the old sink outside the back door. Filling it with cold running water, they would replace the seawater and rinse out as much sand as possible. Then, the cockles were lifted out of the bucket and placed in Granny's biggest saucepan, a batch at a time. The cockles were covered with clean water, brought to the boil and simmered for about five minutes. Once cooked, the shells would spring open, revealing their tasty harvest.

The children would be given a small bowlful at a time, to which they could add vinegar and pepper if they wanted, although they didn't usually bother. They would all sit around on the terrace by the back door eating the warm sea-flavoured treats. The whole process - other than the actual cooking - took place outdoors. For the children, the fact that they could eat what they had just harvested made the cockles taste all the better.

The childhood memory was so strong that Clare got up, determined to book the summer holiday on the Gower that they had all started to talk about on New Year's Day. She wanted her own children to enjoy those same innocent delights that she had loved so much. Why was it that being near the sea gave her a sense of freedom? And freedom from what? Clare couldn't answer this puzzling question. From previous visits, however, she understood how the children reacted when they arrived on the Gower from landlocked Oxfordshire. With around twenty beaches in an Area of Outstanding Natural Beauty, they were spoilt for choice when it came to finding shorelines to explore.

As Clare dressed, she planned some of the activities that she would do with her three children on their summer holiday. She would definitely take them to the pub on the Gower that served Penclawdd Pizzas – a pizza with a topping of bacon, cockles, Welsh cheese, and laver bread, (a local delicacy made of seaweed that tasted like salty spinach). Her mother, Enid, had moved to Penclawdd, as if she had followed those old cockle beds, and would love having her children and grandchildren in the area for their summer holiday.

After getting the children off to school, and walking Pepper, Clare made herself a coffee and got on the phone to her mother. "Darling, how lovely to hear from you!" exclaimed Enid, immediately making Clare feel guilty. When had she last phoned her? Was it that long ago? "Aren't you in work today?"

"No, I don't work in the shop on Wednesday. It's one of my days off, remember?" reminded Clare, stifling a sigh and wondering why her mother always found this little detail of her daughter's life so difficult to remember.

"Nick and I were thinking of coming down to the Gower for the summer, and we don't want to miss the chance of you being there,' she continued. 'Do you have any plans to be away?"

"Well now, let's see…" began Enid. She then started to reel off her coming activities and events.

Goodness, she has more of a social life than I do, thought Clare, as she listened to her mother talking her through her bowls fixture list and rehearsal dates with the local operatic society. Clare would not want it any other way, of course.

Enid had been widowed for two years and had made a great recovery after the initial shock of losing her husband, Howard, from an unexpected heart attack. Clare, Sam, and Lisa had thought that it was quite a good way to go, rather than having a long, lingering illness that dragged on, with the patient gradually becoming frailer and frailer before losing all their faculties. Sam had made the unfortunate mistake of pointing this out to his mother, and got told in no uncertain terms by his recently-widowed mother how tactless a comment this was.

"Well, that's charming that you're glad that your father died quickly," she had snapped at him. "For myself, having lived happily with him for over forty years, I wouldn't have minded nursing him if it meant that I had more time with him. I would actually have quite liked to have had the chance to say goodbye."

With that, she had taken herself upstairs for a cry, leaving Sam feeling rather wrong-footed.

"I was only trying to cheer her up," Sam had told his sisters indignantly. "I thought it would make her feel better, for heaven's sake. Honestly, women are so bloody touchy!"

Two years on, however, and Enid had built up a rich and active solo life. Clare listened to the one-way conversation until her ear started to buzz. Then she cut into her mother's narrative of her social calendar. "So, if we come down for three weeks in August we might actually catch you in at some point?" she joked.

"Of course, dear, of course you will. I wouldn't miss the children for anything! Now, where are you planning to stay? You know you're welcome here."

Enid lived in a tiny stone cottage, which was perfectly suited to her now that she was widowed and living alone. The thick, stone walls made the house feel cosy, and the rear windows overlooked the salt marshes of the north Gower coastline, providing a constantly-changing vista. Although the cottage was large enough for a weekend visit, with only two bedrooms the children ended up sleeping on sofas and camp beds, so it would not be spacious enough for a three-week summer holiday.

"I was thinking of going to Mumbles again. There's plenty for the children to do there if the weather is wet. Now that they're older they can wander around town on their own. Lisa is thinking that they might come too, but she's waiting for Phil to confirm his work dates, and you know how last minute they can be. The thing is, we need to book early to get the cottages with the sea views."

"Well, that's still lovely and close; only twenty minutes' drive over the Gower Moor."

The conversation continued for another ten minutes before her mother said that she would have to dash as she had to go and help with preparing lunches for the 'oldies' lunch club. This was priceless, as she was going to be 72 on her next birthday!

Clare sat down with the holiday brochure and turned to the page where she had circled the cottages she'd considered being suitable for the family. She had stayed at one or two of them in the past, and knew the town very well, so discounted all the ones away from the sea front. One new inclusion in the brochure caught her eye:

Bay View Cottage
Bay View Cottage is the ideal holiday cottage for a large family. It is located in a lane running alongside the Esplanade, with sea views from the lounge, patio garden and front-facing bedrooms. Downstairs accommodation comprises of a large, open sitting room and dining room, leading to a well-appointed kitchen. From the kitchen there are French doors leading to a large raised patio garden with a seating area. From here there are sweeping views over Swansea Bay.

Upstairs is the master bedroom, two single bedrooms, and a family bathroom. On the second floor is an attic bedroom and separate shower room.

Note of caution:
This is an old fisherman's cottage, so the steps to the attic room are narrow and steep, making it unsuitable for the very young, elderly, or infirm.
Bedding provided.
Dogs welcome.

* * *

Clare's choices were limited by the fact that the cottage had to take dogs, as they all wanted Pepper with them. Well, to be honest, perhaps Nick would rather not have the dog with them, but on this matter he was outnumbered. Clare sighed as she thought of Nick and the holiday. He had not been happy about the announcement she had made to all their friends on New Year's Day, but, as it turned out, only the Taylors had been interested. The others hadn't been able to work up any enthusiasm for the Gower, despite Sam's best efforts. Brigitte and John had booked their planned trip to France, and Daphne and Marcus were heading to Greece for some sun.

"Might as well make the most of their failing economy in Europe," Marcus had joked at their recent barbeque. "Every cloud and all that. And talking of clouds

- it always bloody rains in Wales, anyway!"

Sam had stoutly defended the Welsh climate, but the stats did not lie. It did have a higher rainfall than most places – apart from Manchester, and who went there for a holiday?

Clare remembered the last time the family had booked a cottage in Mumbles. Holly was still in her buggy, so it must have been about five summers ago. It had indeed rained a lot that holiday. At one point they'd sat in the car park at Weobley Castle, and hadn't even been able to see the top of the castle tower.

She sighed. That had not been a successful holiday. Nick had appeared distracted, as if he couldn't wait to get back to work. She remembered trying to broach the subject, without success. "Darling, I worry about you working so hard. You need to use this holiday as an opportunity to wind down and relax."

"I'm fine," he'd snapped back. "I just have a lot on the go at the moment. Please don't nag."

Clare didn't think that showing concern at her husband's workload should be classed as nagging, but she tried not to bring the subject up again. *Maybe that was why he hadn't been keen to go back¸ she thought. Perhaps he too was remembering that holiday? Never mind; that was then, this is now.* She picked the phone up again and carefully pressed the numbers for Mumbles Holiday Cottages. *Fingers crossed that Bay View Cottage isn't booked yet.*

8

The Pool Party

"Last one in's a loser!" shouted Toby as he raced into the aquamarine swimming pool. The pool had been recently built in Duncan and Debs' garden, with an infinity side to make the most of the view.

The couple lived in a rambling Victorian house built from Cotswold stone on Boar's Hill, and their back garden fell away with views overlooking the spires and towers of Oxford in the distance. They also had a pool house, with two changing rooms to avoid taking wet feet onto the original-tiled floors of their house.

Duncan and Debs were hosting an early summer party, and streamers and balloons had been artfully placed to celebrate Duncan's fiftieth birthday. Neither of them were keen gardeners, so the temporary decorations added colour to the surroundings.

"Thank goodness the sun is shining," smiled Clare, always stating the obvious when it came to the weather.

She looked adoringly at her son, Toby, jumping into the pool and dive-bombing the other swimmers who had been innocently bobbing up and down in the turquoise water. She totally overlooked his ASBO-esque behaviour.

"He's been so looking forward to having a swim to cool down," she explained to nobody in particular, as if this justified the soaking he was giving everyone in his vicinity. There were a dozen children altogether, either in the pool or sitting around the edge with their legs dangling in the heated water. They ranged in age from seven to sixteen. Their parents could relax and enjoy themselves without having to take turns as pool attendants, leaving that to the older children.

As Clare was speaking, Gabby emerged from the pool house in a swimsuit that showed off her petite, size-eight figure.

"My goodness, you're not getting in with all those children, are you?" asked Clare in horror. "How brave!"

"I can't resist a heated outdoor pool – a real luxury after a week working in the city," gushed Gabby.

She sashayed past Clare in a revealing, cutaway, black swimsuit. Gracefully stepping into the pool, and watched by most of the men, she began to swim elegantly down the length of the pool, executing a professional-looking overarm stroke, and not appearing to mind that she was getting her hair wet in the process. Sam glanced over admiringly and, not for the first time, thought how lucky he was to have such a glamorous girlfriend. Some of the other men were also thinking how stunning she looked, but had more sense than to make a comment that might be overheard by their wives. They didn't want to leave themselves open to a helping of tongue pie.

Clare poured herself a drink from a laden table and wandered over to where her sister, Lisa, was chatting to Debs. This was the first time that the friends had all been outside together since the barbecue when Daphne had taken Marcus' wine. Clare wondered what the men would do today to ensure they kept their hands on the expensive stuff. *Boys will be boys*, she thought indulgently. She was happy enough with her spritzer. Lisa, however, was not prepared to let the matter be forgotten. In a huddle with Daphne, she plotted some wheeze that involved pouring an ordinary wine into one of Duncan's decent decanters and seeing whether the men noticed. Daphne walked into the house to see whether Debs could be persuaded to provide them with a suitably expensive-looking decanter. She returned through the French windows with an innocent look on her face, and winked at Lisa. She glanced around the garden to see who was where, then announced that she might take a dip in the pool. The decanter was left temporarily on the side, forgotten.

"Isn't it wonderful to have a week off work when the forecast is for sunshine and the weather men have actually got it right for once?" Lisa sighed. "Such bliss!"

"Well, not for me, actually. I don't work in education, if you remember, so half term is difficult for me," Clare replied tartly.

Lisa had recently changed jobs and was working as an administrator at Oxford University where she had a generous leave package, working term-time only. *She knows full well that I'm working this week in the shop,* thought Clare. *Honestly, she's as bad as Mum.* In fact, Lisa's mind was on other things. She had been watching Ellen sitting on the edge of the pool, and was wondering whether to share with Clare the news that Ellen was dyslexic. Not that it mattered one jot, but Lisa's competitive nature transformed the information into a kind of failure on Ellen's part.

Clare was feeling unusually sorry for herself. The forecast had indeed predicted warm, dry weather all week, but she would be working for four of those days. Brigitte needed to visit some clothes exhibitions to purchase stock for the winter season, so Clare was in charge of the shop for the week. If she wanted to, she could have asked Brigitte to find someone else to replace her, but she was looking forward to being in charge for a change, so she had said yes right away. She hadn't known then how idyllic the weather was going to be.

Before having the children, Clare had worked for *Oxfam* in Oxford in the Campaigns Department. She had loved the work, and enjoyed the feeling that she was making a difference. But, once the children had come along, just the thought of trying to organise childcare around the journey into work had seemed so daunting that she and Nick had agreed that her career could wait until the children were older. After that, she had never really got back on the promotional ladder. Nick had recently started to suggest she look for something more… what did he call it… *worthwhile?* But there weren't that many job opportunities in a small market town such as Abingdon, and she wouldn't want to commute into Oxford again.

It's not as if we need the money, she consoled herself.

Lisa, by contrast, had taken very little time off when she'd had her girls. Her full-time job – and income – was more important to her. Clare knew that Lisa thought she wasted her degree working in the shop, which perhaps was true, but at the end of the working day Clare walked home with no cares in the world. She would much rather that, than the old days of panics over budgets, working lunches, and unpaid overtime. Besides, she knew that because of her part-time job she had more time to concentrate on keeping up with demands made on her time by the children and Nick. *What did they call it? A work-life balance. Yes, my life is nicely balanced – apart from this week!*

"Mum's coming up on the train tomorrow, remember?" Clare reminded Lisa.

Clare had asked her mother to stay and keep an eye on the children.

"You must bring Sophie and Ellen over one day to see her, and arrange for her to visit you."

The children were old enough to manage on their own, as Sally was a mature 15-year-old. But, since Enid had been widowed two years ago, she liked to visit her grandchildren in Abingdon from time to time for a change of scene. In reply to Clare's suggestion, Lisa pulled out her diary and started running through the various clubs and events she had signed her girls up to for the week, trying to find a free day for them to visit their grandmother. *Poor things*, thought Clare. *By the sound of it, they'll be doing more in their holidays than in a school week.*

The sun continued to blaze down on the garden, and

groups had started to find shade under trees and awnings. Suddenly, there was an outburst of barking. Baxter, Duncan's border terrier, had spotted a neighbour's cat sunning herself in a quiet corner of the large garden. Baxter was incensed. Didn't that cat realise that this was dog territory? Baxter set off at the dog equivalent of an Olympic 100-metre dash to remind the cat of this fact, but, in his haste, forgot about the new pool standing between him and his enemy. He ran straight over the edge of the pool, and just for a moment hovered above the surface. His little legs were still galloping, even though there was no ground beneath them. After the briefest of moments, with Baxter frantically cycling in mid-air, his dogged propulsion was overcome by Newton's Law. Little Baxter found himself plunging into the pool, and had to quickly remember how to do doggy paddle. With much shrieking and laughter from the children, he was quickly retrieved, hoicked out of the pool by Duncan, and wrapped in a big towel to dry.

"Och, stupid wee mutt," said Duncan fondly, towelling the dog's dripping fur.

Baxter hoped he would get a biscuit, on the basis of saving his owner from a dastardly feline. Lisa looked on with disdain. She didn't approve of pets. They made far too much mess and gave nothing in return. *And don't even start with the vet's bills.* After much pleading from her girls, she had relented and bought them a gerbil each, but that was it – no more!

"That reminds me," Lisa turned to Clare. "Does your Mumbles cottage take pets? I assume you want to take Pepper?" Pepper always went away with the family on U.K. holidays.

"Oh, yes. I can't imagine going on holiday without him. He'll love it there. Morning walks on the promenade and afternoons splashing in the sea. You know how he loves paddling in water."

"Mmm…" Lisa knew only too well. She made a

mental note to check that her cottage did *not* take pets. She didn't want to be cleaning up after his sandy paws all the time, thank you very much.

Duncan had finished drying off Baxter, and went back to opening more bottles of wine, while Debs went to the pool to call the children in to collect their food. She started to dish out salads and savouries to the hungry, dripping queue of youngsters before feeding the adults. Clare looked around for Nick to see if they were going to sit together to eat, but he was no longer standing where she had last noticed him talking about football with John and Marcus. She shrugged and carried on chatting to Lisa, and then Gabby joined them from the pool, wrapped in a large beach towel.

Clare stood up and went to join Debs to help dish out the food at one of the large garden tables. As she did so, she saw Nick re-join the others. He had changed into his swimming shorts, so must have been planning to take a dip after lunch. She smiled and gave a wave in his direction, but he appeared not to have noticed her as he re-joined John and Marcus. *Never mind*, she thought, *I'll take him over a plate of his favourite salads with some ham*, and did just that. With her back turned, she didn't notice Daphne, with a sarong draped over a swimsuit, slip out of the pool room and go to sit with Lisa and Gabby.

9

The Long Drive

"...and queues heading westbound on the M4 over both the Severn Bridge and the Second Severn Crossing into Wales are now trailing back ten miles..." the radio traffic announcer informed Nick and Clare. This was not helpful as they were already in the stream of hot steaming metal, trapped like passengers on a roller coaster ride stuck at the bottom of a very big roll. Nick was slowly losing his good humour. The family had set off early to avoid the heavy traffic, but still found themselves in the long tailback.

"Fucking hell," Nick swore. He banged his hand in frustration on the steering wheel, accidently setting off the horn. Neighbouring drivers glanced over to see what had caused him to sound off, quickly realising he was venting the same powerlessness that they also felt. They shrugged and raised their eyes in sympathy.

"Never mind," said Clare soothingly, "the cricket commentary will be starting on the radio soon. Shall I put the channel on now?"

Nick glared at her for being so bloody reasonable. He wanted to yell at her, 'This is all your fault!' even though it wasn't. He closed his eyes briefly – after all, the car wasn't going anywhere – and imagined himself in a place he would much rather be: the London flat. Clare interrupted his daydream.

"At least the children are happy," she was pleased to announce. "They'd have been playing up by this time a few years ago."

True enough, they all had their headphones on, like junior astronauts in a space capsule, either listening to music or watching flickering images on their screens.

"I wonder where the others are. I'll give them a ring." Clare phoned Lisa to try and stop her from joining the queue.

"Where are you? We're stuck near the Severn Crossing in a ten-mile tailback."

"So are we, but we are at the back of the queue, so we can still turn off and drive north around Gloucester. Phil wants to, but I don't. What do you think?"

The two navigators discussed the pros and cons of the two routes, while Phil and Nick listened to one side of the conversation, chipping in as they saw fit. The call ended with Lisa ordering Phil to leave the M4 for the alternative route as, even though it was longer, they wouldn't be sitting in a car park.

"Well, John and the others were right," muttered Nick. "We're going to be bloody hours. At this rate it would have been quicker to take Eurostar and drive to the south of France than travel to South Wales. What a bloody joke! And you almost have guaranteed sun there, unlike here, where…"

"Now, come on," said Clare cheerily, as the car moved forward a whole three metres, "the forecast isn't bad for the next fortnight…"

"Exactly! Not bad! *Not bad* is the best we can expect. I don't know why we bother!"

Clare gave up. If he was going to be this moody there was no point trying to reason with him. He was obviously using selective memory to ignore all those times they had sat in overcrowded airports waiting for delayed flights. And there was that terrible holiday in Brittany where they had come home a day early because the rain had been so incessant. That was partly the reason why she had wanted the relative ease of a holiday in the U.K.

Their annual family holidays always started with Nick in a mood, as if he couldn't adjust to full-time family life. She normally ignored his early outbursts, knowing that in two or three days he would start to relax and unwind. Luckily, just then the ball-by-ball cricket commentary was introduced on the radio so Clare had an excuse to bury her head in her book, after re-tuning the balance so she didn't have to listen to the commentary droning on in the speakers on her side of the car. *I'll leave him to his grumpy self. The cricket will calm him down.* Nothing could dampen her enthusiasm. Crossing the Severn made her feel like she was coming home.

Nick ignored the cricket on the radio. With the traffic crawling along at a snail's pace, he thought gloomily about the holiday looming ahead. He was gutted that he wouldn't be in work for three whole weeks, and wondered whether he could make up some kind of excuse to get back for a long weekend. His frustration was that they usually only went away for two weeks but Clare had persuaded him to take the longer break to make the most of their proximity to Enid, Clare's mother.

"The children don't see enough of their granny," she had coaxed him. "It'll be lovely for them."

"If she wants to see them that much she can come and stay with us a bit more often," he had snapped. Clare had slipped into her most reasonable voice. The one Nick thought of as her 'social worker' voice.

"You know it's important for her to keep up her local activities now that she's widowed, and, if you remember, she did come and stay with us in June."

Nick had given up; they had been here before. Certain conversations in a marriage became like a worn tramline, never varying in any way from other side, and this was one. One of Nick's frustrations with Enid's infrequent visits was that if she was more supportive, Clare might look for a better-paid job.

As for Clare, she knew that by not working in a full-time or stress-related job, she could focus her energies on managing the household. Some days she felt like that old cliché of being a taxi driver, running the children here, there, and everywhere.

Here we go again, they thought simultaneously. By mutual consent, they let the topic drop.

Nick's other frustration lay elsewhere. He had been fancying a blow job for several weeks, and neither Clare nor Annabelle would come up with the goods. *Christ, what's the point of having a mistress if she won't do stuff like that? Fair enough with the wife, but really! It was a farce. I can get straight sex at home, for Christ's sake!*

This topic always led Nick to think of Bill Clinton. *My God, he was getting regular blow jobs from a college kid who looked a million dollars and was giving it away for free, and even his wife forgave him.*

He glanced across at Clare, and his face hardened. *When did she last go down on me? Christ, I can't even remember; it was so long ago. Even John Prescott had regular sex - in his office - and he was no looker. Women fell for the power, obviously. What was that fantastic quote by Caroline Aherne when she interviewed Debbie McGee? Something like: 'What first attracted you to the millionaire Paul Daniels?' Yes, that said it all really about some women…* He gazed at the traffic queue ahead in frustration.

Clare had just reached a crucial point in her thriller when Toby piped up: "I need a pee!"

"Tough!" barked Nick. "You'll have to wait."

Toby started to complain, until Nick told him in no uncertain terms that he had no intention of losing his place in the queue of cars. Clare sighed. *Honestly, sometimes Nick can be so unreasonable.* As they neared the toll booths Nick interrupted Clare's reading with a terse demand. "Get your money ready for the toll."

Clare reached down to the ashtray that she used to keep coins in for car parking. It was empty. Remembering that she had used the last coins earlier in the week and had meant to replace them, she dug her purse out of her handbag and opened it. *Not enough.* The toll was £6.50, and she had £3.47. The unstaffed booths annoyingly did not take notes, and Nick was already in one with a cash bin.

"I don't have enough money. Where's your wallet?"

"There's nothing in it. I meant to go to the cashpoint this morning but didn't get round to it."

He had been out last night after work, and hadn't got home until late. He had emptied his coins into his cash bowl as usual, but in the drama of packing this morning had not returned the money to his pocket. Clare had been asleep in bed when he'd returned as she'd wanted an early night. *That's why he's so short-tempered*, she thought. *Lack of sleep*. She twisted around to face the back seats.

"Quick! Who's got some change for the toll?"

The three children all looked at her blankly. For intelligent children they were giving a good imitation of village idiots. They were not used to being asked for money – that was their job to ask of their parents! Clare tried again.

"Come on! We haven't got any change for the toll. You must have something between you, surely?"

Toby shrugged to indicate otherwise, and returned to his computer game, his contribution to the conversation closed.

Sally, who was usually good with money, looked in her purse and found the princely sum of £1.36 in change, and a ten pound note, which was no help.

"Right, that's £4.73. What have you got, Holly?"

Clare looked ahead and saw that there were only two cars between themselves and the toll. Holly opened her backpack and started to fumble around for her purse. Nick had said nothing during this hunt for money, but now he exploded. He turned on Clare.

"Why the hell didn't you remember the toll money before we set out this morning?"

She bit back her retort. *You're the one driving. It's up to you to have the money, isn't it?* She hated arguing in front of the children.

Just in time, Holly pulled three pound coins out of her purse with a flourish.

"Thanks, darling, we'll pay you back when we get to a cashpoint," said Clare, with more relief than Holly realised.

Just in time, she handed the necessary coins to Nick, who flung them into the catch-net with more energy than was needed, and the car set off again to re-join the stream of traffic. *Well really, not even a 'thank you' from him*, fumed Clare. *How rude! He could at least thank the children.*

Three hours after setting off from their Oxfordshire home, they crossed the Severn and pulled into Magor Services, right outside the entrance. Toby sprinted to the toilets, and Holly took Pepper for a walk on a patch of grass. As they all piled back into the car Clare announced, "Only another two hours."

The response was a collective groan. They were unaware of the additional hour they would have to take threading their way through Swansea's summer traffic. Their scheduled three-hour journey actually ended up taking six.

*** *

Despite the travelling, Clare was delighted to be back in Mumbles. When she returned to the car from collecting their holiday-home keys, she was gushing with excitement.

"Oh, isn't it sweet!" she said, as Nick pulled up outside the fisherman's cottage. She didn't care that nobody bothered to reply.

The cottage was ideal – it had sea views, but wasn't on the coast road, which was always busy during summer months. Lisa and Phil's cottage was two minutes away from the harbour, up a winding lane.

Clare and Nick unloaded what appeared to be the entire contents of their home in Abingdon. The children stretched their limbs and tried to look as though they were helping, while really doing as little as possible. They were more interested in the sleeping arrangements. A fight eventually broke out over who was going to have the large attic room, promptly brought to a close by Nick ordering them to "Shut it!"

The children then slunk around the bedrooms until Toby and Holly reluctantly agreed that Sally could have the attic room as she was the oldest.

Clare walked around to check that the cottage had everything they needed. The garden was tiny, the kitchen was small, and there was no off-road parking, yet she thought that the place had great charm. How much of that was due to the sea view out of the front window? The sound of gulls screeching overhead could not be measured, but was surely the reason for her enjoying the little cottage. It felt rather like playing house, as her children had done all those years ago in playgroup.

She started to unpack in the kitchen, putting food and drinks in the fridge and cupboards, and approving of the china and kitchenware that was at her disposal. She started unpacking, and only stopped when Nick appeared at her side asking what she was doing about making a cup of tea. She was about to point out the location of the kettle, but remembered that he *had* done all the driving.

"Let's go over to *Verdi's* for ice-creams, to make up for all those hours in the car," she suggested.

Verdi's was a restaurant and ice cream parlour at the end of Mumbles Esplanade. It had a large, outdoor terrace overlooking the harbour and Swansea Bay, and was only a short walk from the cottage. The family strolled along the familiar route, with Pepper enjoying the opportunity to stretch his legs and sniff at the lamp posts.

A short time later, the family sat in the sunshine on the café terrace and ordered snacks and drinks, while Clare phoned to see where Lisa and Phil had got to. She soon wished she hadn't.

"Nightmare!" said Lisa, using one of her favourite expressions. "I was talking to the girls and took my eye off the road for one minute, so Phil takes a wrong turn. Luckily, I realised when I saw him heading for Abergavenny. Honestly, if it was up to him we'd be in North Wales by now!"

"Oh no!" consoled Clare. "You poor things! I tell you what; we'll wait at *Verdi's* for you, and we'll all eat supper here. It'll be too late to cook by the time you get here, and anyway, you'll be tired. I've picked the keys up to your cottage as it was getting so late."

Phil and Lisa arrived an hour later, collected the keys from Clare, dumped their belongings in their fisherman's cottage, and joined the Taylors on the terrace of the restaurant.

The adults sat drinking in the sea views and absorbing the rocking motion of the waves that they missed so much by living inland. The cousins were more interested in planning visits to the shops along the front. The sisters discussed the cottages, the men discussed their horrendous journeys, and the cousins made plans for the three weeks stretching ahead of them. Pepper sat at their feet, waiting for titbits, listening out for his two favourite words, *walkies* and *biscuits*, and enjoying the unique smell of ozone and seaweed. He didn't mind where he was, as long as his favourite people were with him.

10

The Rainy Day

Clare was laughing. Nick looked up from texting, and asked sourly, "What's so hysterical?"

"Oh, come on… " she replied, pointing to the TV. She was watching one of her favourite programmes, where people sent in videos of themselves with friends, family, and pets; falling over, tripping up, and generally making fools of themselves. Clare knew it was moronic – some of it was even staged – but she couldn't help laughing along. The laughter was a release.

"It's just a bit of fun," she said, feeling the need to justify her enjoyment.

Outside, the rain was dashing down – the first rain they had seen since arriving in Mumbles. That meant the beach was out of the question for once.

The family had been in Bay View Cottage for over a week, and were now fully recovered from the trauma of the drive. They had spent the last few days enjoying the sunshine, and visiting local beaches. Enid had been over for Sunday lunch, and Holly had given her a guided tour of the cottage, exploring it together.

"And this," Holly had said with a flourish, waving her arms dramatically as she opened the door, "is my bedroom. Please enter."

Holly, as the youngest, had been given the smallest room, but she thought that it was perfect. The single bed was placed under the window and she could lie in bed and gaze at the sea beyond the esplanade. She had a little bedside table with a pink lamp that she loved – pink being her favourite colour. She was only seven and had not yet gravitated to the head-to-toe black favoured by the teenage friends of her big sister, Sal. She and her Granny had enjoyed looking out of the window at the boats on the glistening water.

Right now, Holly was sprawled on her bed, engrossed in a book, and waiting for the call for tea.

"I don't see what's so funny about people falling over and getting hurt," replied Nick huffily, going back to his phone.

Sal walked into the room. "What are you watching?" she asked. She recognised the programme and frowned. "Isn't there anything better on?" she sneered.

Clare looked up and wondered why she was in a strop.

"Sit down and join us," she suggested, patting the sofa next to her.

"As if!" Sal said, and stomped out of the room.

Clare sighed. She didn't often request much on TV: the odd detective drama; *Antiques Road Show*; *University Challenge*… She knew that the programme she was watching was totally low-brow, but seeing all the pratfalls was such innocent fun - she hoped no-one really got injured making the videos. After all, slapstick was the basis of some of the greatest comedy of the twentieth century, from Laurel and Hardy to Mr Bean. *So there. I don't need to apologise to anyone for enjoying myself.* Toby slouched into the room, and he also frowned at the TV programme.

"I wanted to watch that talent show," he muttered.

"This programme finishes at seven," Clare replied. "You can choose something to watch then."

He glowered, then skulked out of the room. *It must be the weather*, Clare thought, glancing out of the window at the relentless rain. Then, her thoughts returned to the programme. The current batch of clips showed some unfortunate brides caught on video – most of them falling over on the dance floor on the evening of their wedding day.

The videos reminded Clare of her own wedding day all those years ago. It had been the most wonderful day, although, thinking back, perhaps it was just as well nobody had taken a video of the event. In an attempt to please her gran, she had fallen in with the suggestion of what to sing for her second hymn. When the congregation had stood up to sing *Oh Perfect Love* no one had known the version of the song played by the organist – herself included – and the first verse was played in total silence.

Despite the tension of the occasion, she had realised how farcical this was, especially as the vicar had asked everyone at the start to 'sing their socks off'. A brief consultation had taken place, where it was agreed that the congregation would all sing the first hymn for a second time. Luckily, both Clare and Nick had found it as funny as everyone else. Their shoulders had been shaking as they stood at the front of the church singing *Bread of Heaven* for the second time. Whenever Clare went to a wedding she enjoyed recounting the story, and discovered that nobody else had ever been in the same situation, which only made the story funnier for her.

That was one of the things that had attracted her to Nick. He always used to find humour in most things. In fact, before the children were born they were always laughing, even sometimes when they were making love. She caught herself. *Before the children?* It was true... although she laughed and joked with the children, she and Nick laughed less than they used to. They were both so busy, she guessed, just getting through the rush that was life with three kids. She tried to compare her marriage with that of Lisa and Phil. *They always seem to be arguing, yet have a perfectly successful marriage in every other aspect.*

She returned her gaze to the screen as the final series of clips began to roll.

"Good grief!" snorted Nick. "Cats and dogs. Talk about scraping the bottom of the barrel!"

Clare ignored him and watched as a kitten slid off a

table onto the back of an unsuspecting cat below. The absurdity of the scene set her off giggling again. She loved the way the show enabled her to laugh without any effort. She was reminded of when Baxter had fallen into Duncan's swimming pool. *Shame I didn't film him on my phone. I might have earned two hundred and fifty quid.* Clare looked at her husband, and was pleased to see that he had finally been amused by the animal clips, and was now grinning at the furry fun. As the final credits rolled, she stood up to call Toby to tell him that the TV was free. She left the room smiling, and in just the right frame of mind to prepare supper for the family.

The minute Clare walked out of the room, Nick flicked through the sports channels, looking for something more interesting than home videos. *Jesus, Clare must be losing the plot, watching crap like that*, he thought sourly, forgetting that he had actually been entertained by some of the more stupid clips. As he scrolled down the options, he caught sight of Boris Becker, the German tennis pundit. *Boris Lucky Beggar more like it*, he thought. He was the celebrity who got caught having sex in a store cupboard with a stranger in between courses, while taking his wife out to a sushi restaurant for dinner. *Fantasy sex at its best,* Nick mused.

He and Clare had actually visited the same restaurant in Canary Wharf – one of the famous *Nobu* chain. Brigitte adored sushi, and was sick of John moaning about it. 'God, who thought cold rice and seaweed was edible?' was his favourite response whenever she suggested it, so she had insisted on taking him to a restaurant where he could see it being made to the highest standard. A group of them had gone in the end, Nick only agreeing to go in order to find the infamous 'Boris' cupboard, as his views on sushi were the same as John's.

Once they were at the bar having pre-meal drinks, the wives didn't notice the men needing the toilets more than usual, as they sloped off in turns to find the location of the tryst, but without success. In fact, Nick had bumped into Daphne in the corridor on her way to the loo, and suggested that they try out the same act in the disabled toilet. Not very sexy, he knew, but every opportunity… *Good old Daphne, she was a good sport like that.* To her, sex was just a physical workout, like an hour down the gym.

Daphne had drunk so much that by the time the dessert menu was offered, she mistook one of the digestif after-dinner drinks on the menu for a pudding with digestive biscuits. When the drink was placed in front of her she complained to the waiter that it was rather runny for a pudding.

"Call this a pudding? You could drink it!" she informed him, thinking she was being witty.

"You are quite right," the waiter agreed, with consummate professionalism, and brought her a plate of *petite fours* on the house, which they all shared.

"That's more like it," slurred Daphne, tucking into the tiny chocolates.

Pissed as usual, thought Nick, *and no wonder – this bloody food wouldn't feed an infant. Anyway, the only reason the public knew about Becker's dalliance was because the woman had become pregnant and demanded a huge pay out. So, maybe not such a great sexual fantasy after all.*

Toby broke into his reverie. "Pass the remote, Dad. *X Factor* is on and Mum said we could watch it."

He flicked to the channel and slumped down next to his father. Clare walked back in from the kitchen half an hour later, to see Nick and Toby slouched on one sofa, with Sally and Holly on the other, all gazing at the TV screen. *Happy families*, she smiled to herself. *I'll serve supper in front of the TV rather than interrupt them, now that they're all back in a good mood.*

She didn't think to wonder who Nick was texting.

11

Langland Bay

"Ah, this is more like it," sighed Nick as he took a swig from his pint of chilled lager and admired the view. He and Phil were standing on the balcony of the *Langland Brasserie*, looking out over the rocking tide that was offering free lapping therapy to all-comers. The brasserie had only been built recently, and was a welcome addition to the bay, which, in the past, had only held a traditional cafe and bucket and spade shop. The restaurant's raised balcony was built right over the sand, and the shady terrace meant that you could sit out, even on showery days. It was painted a tasteful Mediterranean blue and there was a wood-burning stove inside for colder days.

Langland Bay was only a couple of miles along the coast from Mumbles, and was a favourite watering hole for the two men. Langland was made up mainly of summer homes and holiday lets, with neat rows of pine-green beach huts along the south side, and busy tennis courts at the rear. The beach was busy during summer months, but usually quiet and peaceful in the evenings when all the day-trippers had disappeared.

The sun was setting over the cliffs and the men were enjoying a pint after a day of waiting on the demands of their children and wives. The day was ending with a casual supper at Bay View Cottage. The men had left Clare and Lisa drinking rosé on Lisa's patio, with the children indoors fanned around the TV.

Nick found an empty table on the balcony, on the side overlooking the bay, and sat down before taking a look around to take in his fellow drinkers. *Christ, you could even kid yourself you're in the South of France with this view and bar.* He remembered years ago when he and Clare had travelled to the French Riviera. He had insisted on visiting St. Tropez in the remote hope that he might bump into Brigitte Bardot. Not surprisingly that hadn't happened. *Now, she was really a looker, and so sexy with it. Hadn't she gone a bit nuts? Kept hoards of dogs and voted for Le Pen?* His reverie was interrupted by some laughter coming from another table at the end of the balcony. He turned from the neon orange sunset to see who was making the noise.

"I see Trinny and Susanna are in this evening," Nick murmured to Phil, nodding to the table in the corner. Nick had a habit of naming fellow drinkers after famous people so he could talk about them without having to bother about being discreet. Phil turned to look, and saw two ladies sharing a bottle of chilled white wine with weekend papers strewn across the table.

"Which one are you having?" joked Phil, who had no intention of making a play at the two women.

Nick, however, gave the question serious thought. Probably not 'Susanna'; she looked too much like Clare – slightly chunky, with hair pulled back into a pony tail. *No point eating out what you have at home, after all. What did Paul Newman say? Why go out for a burger if you've got steak at home? Mind you, he was married to Joanne Woodward who was a beautiful actress and looked as though she had fun in the sack.* 'Trinny,' on the other hand, was elegant and slim, with stylish clothes and some expensive-looking jewellery. Nick liked a woman who bothered about her looks. Nice sun-streaked hair, too. He turned to Phil.

"Trinny, I think. Sorry, Phil, you get the mate!" He roared at his joke and took another quaff of lager.

Phil laughed along, then lost interest and started talking about football. Nick continued to absorb the lovely view - the sea and the women - when another group walked onto the balcony. A mature couple with a young boy of around Toby's age strolled across to where Trinny and Susanna were sitting. They exchanged greetings and were invited to join the table. Papers were swished aside and another bottle of wine appeared.

"Blimey, we've got Fred and Ginger joining them now," Nick reported to Phil.

"Good call," acknowledged Phil. The man was small, trim, and dapper, like Fred Astaire, and his wife had auburn curls.

"And Jonathan Creek," Phil added, referring to the mop of curls sported by the young boy.

Phil was quite pleased with his attempt at naming the boy – that was usually Nick's forté. As Nick went to the bar to collect two more pints, he tried to make eye contact with Trinny, but she was having too much fun chatting to the group around the table. When he returned, the decibel count had risen considerably at the corner table as the wine flowed. He handed Phil his pint. As he did so Phil exclaimed, "Well, I'll be… What's she doing here?"

Phil stood up from the table without explanation and approached a group of four women who had just sat down at the last free table. One of them shrieked when she saw him and threw her arms around him. Nick looked on in astonishment, and not without a little envy. She had a look of Julia Roberts about her – very nice indeed.

It was usually Nick that left Phil in the lurch when they went out for a drink. He didn't enjoy being dumped without an explanation. He sat and nursed his pint, grateful that at least he could watch the fun on the corner table. He heard Jonathan call Fred 'Grandad', which explained his relationship with Fred and Ginger. Yet another bottle of wine was opened. The young lad sat quietly, making a show of reading a book, while the adults laughed at seemingly nothing very funny – at least to him, anyway. After a while, Susanna decided to bring him into the conversation by suggesting a game of 'Name that Cartoon Song'. Jonathan looked baffled.

"I don't know any cartoon songs," he admitted.

"Don't be silly. Of course you do. Everyone does!" she pronounced. "Think of Disney."

He looked uncomfortable, and remained silent. Suddenly she started dum-dum-dumming the theme tune of *The Flintstones*, without the words. The boy looked perplexed and slightly embarrassed. When Susanna had finished, she looked at him expectantly.

"I don't know it," he confessed, looking like he was about to cry.

With that, Susanna burst into song with the words to the first verse of *The Flintstones*. When she finished, the group laughed and applauded. Fred Astaire looked at her with admiration.

"You've got a great voice there," he said admiringly. "I've always read that the Welsh are good singers." She gave him a teasing look.

"Slight difference: the Welsh just *think* that they can sing." Susanna laughed, pleased with the compliment despite decrying her skills.

Ginger looked slightly miffed at this flirty exchange, and moved the subject on. The young lad sat in silence, looking as though he had failed some important exam. Susanna seemed to feel sorry for him.

"Come on!" she ordered. "Let's go and buy you an ice cream to help you to recover from your ordeal."

The offer made him smile with delight. She marched him into the restaurant to buy an ice cream, which quickly restored him to his former good-natured self. As she passed his table, Nick looked her over. *At least she has a sense of humour.* He considered hanging around and speaking to her later. As he was musing on this thought, Phil returned to the table and explained his absence.

"You'll never guess who that was! Only Tasha - my first great love. God, we were the original Romeo and Juliet, and only broke up when she went to university – it broke my heart." Nick didn't like to point out that they actually hadn't been the original Romeo and Juliet. That had been Romeo and Juliet.

He turned and sized up the foursome. Apart from Tasha, the other three weren't particularly eye-catching. They looked like extras from *Coronation Street*. *Never mind, beggars can't be choosers,* he thought with a shrug. *And beer goggles work better than any expensive face creams.*

"Why don't we join them? It might be a bit of a laugh," suggested Nick.

* * *

By the time both men had returned home some hours later, Clare had turned in for an early night, but Lisa was sitting up waiting for Phil.

"Where on earth have you been 'til now? I thought you were only popping out for a quick pint?" she demanded crossly.

"You'll never guess!" said Phil innocently. "I only bumped into Tasha from school. She's down here for a week's holiday…"

Lisa cut him off. "What? I'm sitting here babysitting your children while you're out chatting up an ex-girlfriend? Well, thanks very much!" The relaxed hours chatting in the balmy evening air in the garden and drinking chilled rosé with Clare were quickly forgotten.

"No, not chatting her up, just catching up…" he explained, but Lisa hadn't finished.

"Catching up? Catching up! Catching up with what?"

Phil sighed. It was so long ago that he and Tash had been an item that it didn't occur to him that Lisa would be jealous. But Lisa held the opinion that the more space you allowed men to misbehave, the more opportunities they took – and tonight proved the point. Not content with one of the pubs in Mumbles, they had chosen to drive over to Langland, and look what had happened.

"And another thing," she continued, becoming angrier by the minute. "I've been asking you to take us there for a meal since we arrived, and you can't even be bothered, yet off you swanned tonight when Nick clicked his fingers."

"You know that's not my fault," Phil replied. "Nick never wants to go with the family because he'll end up paying for the three kids and Toby will probably leave half his food…" he trailed off, realising how feeble his excuse sounded.

"We're not joined at the hip!" she snapped. "We can quite easily go without them. We don't need permission! If they don't want to come, they don't have to!"

"Right, let's go there tomorrow," suggested Phil pleadingly. But it was too late. Lisa wanted to play the martyr. She stomped upstairs to the airing cupboard and found some bedding, which she threw on the sofa.

"There you go," she stormed. "You like the bachelor life. You can have the sofa to yourself. Enjoy!" She marched upstairs to bed to lie awake, wondering how Tasha had aged. Meanwhile, Phil fell straight off to sleep, after cursing himself for opening his big mouth.

12

Bracelet Bay

Another sunny day in Paradise, thought Clare as she opened her eyes to bright sunshine beaming through a gap in the curtains. The bedroom had been styled in seaside red, white, and blue, with anchor motifs on the curtains and bedspreads. It was the end of the second week of their holiday and both families had fallen into a routine that pleased everyone.

The children liked to go to a beach for most of the day, then wander around Mumbles town in the late afternoons and early evenings. Clare and Lisa both cooked as little as possible, feeding everyone up with picnics, barbeques, pub lunches, and occasional meals out. The men went for their early evening drink while the sisters stayed with the children and planned the following day's outing.

Clare lazed, and started planning meals for the day. She would have to stock up at the local supermarket before they left, unless they had another pub lunch. Luckily, the sunny weather meant that salads were popular, and they were easy to prepare. As she lay there, wondering what the family might do that day, the decision was made for her by Holly who came running into the bedroom.

"Come on, Lazybones. We're waiting for you!" Clare hadn't noticed that Nick had already left her side. She must have slept more heavily than usual in the bracing sea air.

"Where's your father?" she asked sleepily as she to pulled on her faded denim shorts and stripy t-shirt. She was loving that she didn't have to think about looking smart – one of the many free luxuries of a bucket-and-spade holiday!

"He's downstairs. We've all been up for ages. Daddy says we can go to the rock pools in Bracelet Bay, so come on!"

Without waiting for a reply, Holly sprinted downstairs to tell the others that their wait was over. Sure enough, when Clare descended the narrow staircase, the children were sitting on the squashy sofas surrounded by beach bags and shrimp nets. She smiled at Nick.

"Hi, Early Bird. Sure you don't mind?" Clare asked him.

Bracelet Bay was Nick's least favourite beach as it was always crowded and therefore often littered with leftover bottles, cans, and plastic bags. The children loved it, however, because it was within walking distance of the cottage. There was also a café serving refreshments and, best of all, the walk ran alongside rock pools full of sea life.

Nick smiled and shrugged. "Just this once won't be too painful, I guess. Low tide is in the middle of the day, to make the most of the rock pools. I've told the others and we're going to meet them down there. I've been to the supermarket, so we've got food in for lunch."

After his late night he thought it was a good idea to keep in Clare's good books, but she didn't even mention him returning home after she had turned in for the night. She made sure that the loo had been visited, swimming costumes and towels were packed, with her own bag full of all the additional beach essentials: sun cream, insect cream, plasters, sunglasses, sun hats, bottles of water, and kitchen sink. The children struggled into their wetsuits. Even on sunny days the sea could be cold, and they enabled them to spend longer in the chilly waters of Swansea Bay.

As they were heading for the door Clare turned to

Pepper who was sitting hopefully. "Sorry, darling, you won't be able to come," she told him, leaning down to stroke his silky head.

Pepper had to stay at the cottage, as dogs weren't allowed on Bracelet Bay in high season. That was another reason why they didn't go there often. He had already had his morning run on the promenade, pee-mailing the other dogs with a little tinkle on the lamp posts. The family planned to return home for lunch, to let him out. Toby gave him a big hug and ordered him to his basket, knowing full well that by the time the front door closed he would be jumping on the sofa to look for them out of the window.

In a painfully slow procession, rather like royalty progressing around the country in times gone by, they headed down to the promenade. Bracelet Bay was the first beach around the headland from Mumbles, so it was only a fifteen-minute walk around the cliffs past the pier. It was only a small cove, but the rock pools, and its close location to the town, made it popular with families.

As it was still only mid-morning, the large car park was almost empty when they walked through it, but Clare knew that by early afternoon it would be full. A lot of the cars would only stop for a short time, with the occupants pausing for an ice cream from the apple-shaped shop on the headland, or for a cup of tea from the café, before heading off to some of the other beauty spots on the Gower.

The steps leading down to the beach were steep and uneven. Clare supposed that sitting in cars without even getting down on the beach was an age thing as it was a difficult climb down, and even more difficult to walk back up. Clare slowly followed the family down the steps to where the sand met the rocks.

By the time her sandals touched the warm sand, the children had dropped their possessions in a jumbled heap and had run straight into the sea. She spread her towel out and sat down, opening her bag ready to start the routine of smothering herself with sun cream. Nick lay down next to her and had read barely one sentence of his summer blockbuster before Lisa and her girls turned up.

"Good timing!" exclaimed Clare. "We've only just sat down."

Lisa dropped her things on Clare's free side, and chivvied her two girls into laying out their towels before they could follow their cousins into the sea. Eventually they were gone, dashing down to jump the waves.

"Thank goodness – peace at last!" sighed Lisa. "They've been like a pair of seagulls fighting over a sandwich this morning. They can stay in the water all morning as far as I'm concerned."

As she started to spray oil over herself, Lisa recounted her latest tale of woe. Phil had been phoned last night and asked to do a studio session in Abbey Road, so had set off at dawn to avoid rush hour traffic along the M4 to London. He expected to be back in a day or two.

"I know the money's good," moaned Lisa, "but it spoils the holiday when he goes off like this."

She didn't share the story with her sister, but she was also fretting that they had parted following a quarrel that she had started but could do nothing about now.

Nick, who was only half listening, felt sorry for the bloke. It seemed to him that Phil could do no right in Lisa's eyes. If Phil worked, he was at fault for not being around to help with the children, and if he was home Lisa moaned about him getting under her feet and not bringing home the bacon. He sighed loudly without realising it. *Some people!* She had chosen to marry him, after all, knowing that he was a musician and that his life would probably be this way. For most musicians it was a hand-to-mouth existence, unless of course they were one of the few that broke through to the top ranks of stardom.

His mind drifted, wondering what it would be like to be someone as famous as Mick Jagger. *Hmm… travelling the world, villa in the South of France, membership at Lords Cricket Club, unlimited beautiful women throwing themselves at me. Did Jagger still sleep with groupies, or did he mix with a better sort of fan now that he was a pensioner? Jerry Hall had turned a blind eye to his philandering for years. Although, his life had taken a turn for the worse recently, when this new one had gone and killed herself. Bad show… No, I wouldn't want that nightmare hanging over me.*

With his daydream punctured by reality, he returned to his blockbuster while Lisa continued to dump on Clare, only occasionally pausing for breath to check that she could see the girls and shout instructions at them. Nick wouldn't have been surprised to see her turn up on the beach with binoculars – anything to keep her eyes on her two girls. His mind drifted back to the *Rolling Stones*, to ponder how he would cope with life on the road as a rock star. As he did so, he allowed the shushing of the distant waves to lull him to sleep and help him recover from his late night.

In that way, the morning drifted pleasantly by, with occasional interruptions from the children for drinks and ice creams. Toby eventually decided he was hungry, and broke into Nick's snooze with over-loud demands for lunch.

"Come on!" he pleaded. "It must be lunch time. I'm starving!"

A group decision was made to head back to the cottages for lunch. Once again, beach gear had to be collected, towels shaken and rolled away, and beach bags filled. Sal and Sophie led the way back to town, holding their sandals ready to put on in the car park, away from the sand. Sophie had also retrieved her mobile from her mother, and looked as if she was about to take a selfie in her wetsuit. She had only walked about a hundred metres, when she shrieked and collapsed onto the sand. Sal bent over and saw what the problem was.

"Oh no," she groaned, holding up a shard of glass. "Some idiot has left a broken bottle here."

She started to pick pieces up and put them in a plastic bag that Clare found for her. After that, she carried the fragments with her until she could put the bag in a public bin.

"Bloody litter louts!" fumed Nick. "This is why I never want to come to this beach."

"Well, if you hadn't been on that blessed phone…" Lisa started to accuse Sophie, but Clare put a restraining hand on her arm. Poor Sophie was trying to staunch the blood with an old tissue and looking most woebegone.

"Well, that cut will need cleaning and stitching," declared Clare, taking control of the mini-drama. "Nick, could you run back and fetch the car and drive Sophie and Lisa to hospital? I'll take the others back to the cottage and give them lunch."

Nick did as suggested and loped back to the cottage for the car keys, while the others helped Sophie to limp up to the car park to wait for his return. Clare saw his receding figure disappear down the road, grateful that he had taken charge, not realising that it was actually she who had choreographed the solution.

Nick returned ten minutes later with the car to take Sophie to hospital. He suggested that Lisa wasn't needed. He couldn't bear the thought of her fussing over nothing at the hospital. But Lisa insisted on accompanying her daughter, and Sal went along to keep her cousin company.

Clare, Toby, Holly, and Ellen returned to Bay View Cottage where Clare laid out a spread of sandwiches and pies for the remaining hungry children. The others had still not returned from hospital two hours later, so rather than return to Bracelet Bay, Clare suggested that the children take Pepper for a cliff-top walk. The three youngsters promptly agreed.

As Toby left with Pepper pulling on the lead, followed by Holly and Ellen, Clare called to Holly.

"Remember to look for things for your holiday scrapbook!"

When they were younger, all the children had put together scrapbooks about their summer holidays, although Holly was the only one who still did it. She would collect brochures, till receipts, car park tickets, and anything else to show where they had visited that day, then stick them all into a big scrapbook. It had been a wonderful way to pass an hour or two on wet afternoons or in the evenings while the kids were waiting for their evening meal to be prepared.

Once the children had left for their walk, Clare sat outside on the small back patio with a pleasant feeling of having nothing to do, and no-one to worry about. She read her book until Nick eventually returned from the hospital, just as the sun was moving around the headland and leaving her in the shade.

He headed straight for the fridge. "God, I need a beer after that. It was a nightmare," he started to tell Clare. "It took half an hour just to get to the hospital, because of the traffic. Then we had to wait for two hours just to be seen. Lucky we went, though! They cleaned her up, put in three stitches and gave her a tetanus injection, just to be on the safe side."

He scavenged in the fridge as he recounted the afternoon, and found some pork pies to wolf down as a very late lunch.

"Oh, well, I'll go and get all the gory details," said Clare, putting her book down regretfully. "The others are due back from their walk with Pepper any time now. Are you alright here if I leave you on your own to wait?"

Nick hadn't heard the question – he was already trying to tune the TV to the cricket.

"I guess that's a 'yes' then," Clare murmured to herself as she headed for the front door.

She found Lisa sitting in her kitchen with a glass of white wine in front of her.

"Nightmare," said Lisa, repeating Nick.

She nodded to the fridge, indicating for Clare to pour herself a glass of wine, and proceeded to take Clare through every stage of what appeared to be the most routine of surgical procedures in far more detail than Clare needed, or indeed wanted. Lisa was making a drama out of what was the sort of boring hospital visit that Clare had made with her own children on many occasions. *What mother is lucky enough to avoid a visit to Outpatients with their children?* None that Clare knew. She remembered her most recent visit – taking Toby for stiches in his thigh when a stud had caught him when playing rugby. He still carried the scar.

Lisa was now in full flow. She poured them both a second glass of chilled Pinot. As Lisa chattered on, Clare only half listened, observing – as she often did – how very different they were, both physically and mentally. Lisa had long, luxurious brown hair that she tinted auburn, while Clare's was shoulder length and nondescript. Lisa was tall and athletic looking, although she did very little exercise. This had always annoyed Clare, who loved sport but, because of her lack of height, struggled to succeed at many of the games that she tried.

She sighed, and wondered how long Lisa was going to moan for. She was typically cup half-empty, unlike Clare's more positive, sunny nature.

The conversation moved on to Phil's absence, and how he should have been there for the domestic crisis. *Poor Phil, even when he doesn't do anything wrong, he's still found wanting! What hope is there for the two of them? Lisa seems so dissatisfied.* Clare couldn't help comparing how practical Nick was compared to Phil. Even if Phil had been around, he wouldn't have dealt with the matter in the unflappable way that Nick had. *Lucky me!*

Clare walked to the fridge for a refill, wondering what to make for supper. One thing the sisters did have in common was a fondness for white wine.

As she sat back down, her phone pinged with a text from Nick.

It read: *I'm going to buzz off for a drink for an hour to recover.*

She smiled and texted back: *You've earned it x.*

Back in Bay View Cottage, Nick smiled at Clare's text and put his phone safely in his pocket. The children had returned from their walk and were now spread out on the comfy sofas watching TV. They would not stir until they were presented with food by their mother, other than to raid the kitchen cupboards for snacks before then. He said goodbye and drove up to *Langland Brasserie*, where he had an appointment with 'Susanna', real name Nia.

13

The Birthday Party

Toby got up earlier than usual as it was his birthday and he was desperate to open his presents. He ran into his parents' bedroom, saw that they were giving every indication of being fast asleep, but chose to ignore their ruse. Being a teenager at last meant he could ignore such things.

"Hey, it's your favourite child!" he shouted, bouncing on the end of the bed. Nick played possum as Clare opened her eyes at the noise.

She groaned "What time is it?"

"Birthday o'clock! I'm a teenager! I can bloody swear!" shrieked Toby. "And Pepper is waiting to see my presents." Pepper agreed by wagging his tail, almost knocking over Clare's flimsy side table. In all the excitement, he forgot his manners and leapt onto the bed to join in the action.

"Get that damned dog off the bed!" growled Nick, revealing the fact that he too was awake.

Pepper knew that Nick meant business and jumped down from the bed. *Fleeting pleasures*, thought Pepper.

Clare sat up with a sigh, knowing that they would get no peace until Toby had opened his presents that she had hidden out of his sight. Toby had asked for a new computer game that Clare had bought, even though she thought he spent too much time playing them. She had bowed down to his pestering and bought the latest, violent shoot-em-up that he wanted. *Super Nanny wouldn't think much of that!* she thought regretfully, as she handed Toby the package.

She had also bought some juggling balls for him, as it was one of his latest crazes, and at least kept him fit. There were also vouchers and cards from friends and family. Toby opened them with enthusiasm, handing the cheques back to his mother for safekeeping, and left the cards and envelopes where they fell.

He ran downstairs to feed Pepper and put him in the garden, with strict instructions from Clare not to wake the girls, otherwise they would be cranky all day.

Luckily, Holly woke shortly after Toby had fed the dog, so he had someone to share his over-active good mood with. With great difficulty she had managed not to blurt out that his present from her was a new collar for Pepper, something that they would both get the pleasure out of using. He acted suitably pleased and immediately changed Pepper's old collar for the new one.

"Nice one, Sis," he thanked her, once it was round Pepper's neck.

* * *

The house members gradually surfaced. They all walked across to *Verdi's* for a birthday brunch.

The plan for the day was for everyone to travel to Llangennith for a beach barbeque at Rhossili Bay. The forecast was sunny, so they would spend the day on the vast expanse of sand on the other side of the Gower – the beach with the best surf. They had already visited it several times this holiday. Several hours were spent, sat out on *Verdi's* terrace, enjoying the warm rays.

Clare phoned Lisa and Sam to tell them where they were.

Sam and Gabby had driven down the night before to enjoy a long weekend out of London and share in the birthday celebrations. The couple had purposely not booked anything earlier in the year, banking on getting a last minute cancellation. There were not many short rentals available only for the weekend at high season, so a cancellation was the easiest way to book one. Sure enough,

Sam's usual good luck had held and the love-birds had been able to hire a small flat right on the sea front, just a short walk from the other two cottages.

Sam and Gabby strolled onto *Verdi's* terrace shortly after the phone call, Sam carrying a box almost as tall as himself. Gabby sat down in a neon-yellow sundress with matching jacket and designer sunglasses, looking far too sophisticated for a day on the beach in South Wales. *The front of a fashion magazine would be more appropriate for that outfit*, thought Clare enviously.

Sam handed the huge box to Toby. "Happy Birthday, Captain," he joked as he handed it over. Toby looked at the image on the side of the box that Sam hadn't bothered to wrap.

"Oh, wow," beamed Toby. "An inflatable boat. Cool!"

Sam had given more thought than usual to his nephew's present, which very often consisted of just money. He was a dealer in the city where competition was taken for granted in all aspects of life, not only in the workplace. He and his colleagues constantly tried to outdo each other, and bragging was second nature to them. He had bought the expensive rubber dingy more to impress them than Toby. When he realised that some of the guys knew the Gower, and sometimes surfed there, he had talked up the weekend.

"Yeah, we're off surfing for a few days," he had informed them. "I've checked the weather and the surf should be good."

He only ever body boarded, but didn't feel the need to make this distinction. His colleagues had assumed he was talking about standing surfing, and were grudgingly impressed. As the conversations became more detailed, and costs of boards cropped up and Sam surreptitiously googled the necessary information he needed. He'd forgotten that his colleague, Elliott, regularly surfed in Newquay, Cornwall. *Shit!* But he'd got away with it.

He also hoped to impress Gabby with his generosity, but she was more interested in the view than Toby's present. She was leaning on the rails, gazing out over the harbour. Half a dozen small boats were bobbing gently on the calm tide.

"This is just too sweet," she cooed, as she looked out over the bay, the sea twinkling with sunbursts on the waves.

Sam left the family group and joined her. "Just like you, sweetheart," he whispered, putting his arm around her shoulders. "If you think this is good, wait 'til you see the beach we're heading for."

Once Lisa and the girls turned up, they ate their brunch, then trooped back to their cottages to load up for the day out. Three carloads of body boards, wetsuits, barbeques, food, and the new boat crossed the moor from one side of the Gower to the other, heading for Rhossili Bay. By the time they had parked and carried all their possessions from the car park over the sand dunes to the open beach, the adults were ready for a lie down. If Pepper had the brain cells to rank his favourite beaches in order, this would have probably been number one. He could chase over the sand dunes and run himself ragged on the miles of sand, before splashing in the shallows of the crystal blue water that had no rocks to hurt his paws.

"Is it really worth all this effort?" complained Lisa who didn't have Phil to help her carry all the paraphernalia. Her comments were ignored. She lay out her beach towel, seemingly oblivious to the dramatic seascape that nature was providing.

The others definitely felt that it was worth the trek. The views were spectacular, with the headland of Worms Head on one side, and the Carmarthenshire coast in the distance on the other. Out on the broad blue Bristol Channel, miniature tankers took forever to edge out of sight. Occasional white clouds drifted overhead, with a pale blue sky behind them, washed out by the hot sun.

Black-headed terns twisted on the gusts of cooler air that prevented the day from becoming uncomfortably hot.

General mayhem ensued after the children were covered in sun cream and sent off to the water's edge, despite them being given strict instructions not to lose their fix on where the group was sitting. The strong currents made it easy for swimmers to drift along the beach without realising, so they used a coastguard mast behind them as a landmark. It was high tide, but even so, the water was a distance from the group. Clare gave Toby a safety talk about tides, warning him not to row too far out. Sam and Toby found the pump, and between them they pumped the boat full of air. They followed the girls down to the sea, Toby carrying the two oars and Sam burdened by the yellow and blue boat over his broad shoulders. Holly ran up to them.

"Can I have a go?" she asked.

"No! It's *my* birthday and *my* boat, so *you* can buzz off," Toby answered with typical brotherly love.

Sam took his trainers off away from the water's edge to hold the boat while Toby climbed in, closely followed by Holly who clambered in as well, totally ignoring Toby's earlier comment. He realised it might be more fun after all with a companion, so he ordered her to the other end, and started rowing. He paddled along to where the other girls were bodyboarding. They all wanted to have a go, so they spent the rest of the morning taking it in turns to row along the edge of the sea, or pull each other using the rope.

Clare regularly glanced up from where she was lying on her towel, reading her third novel of the holiday. She had bought a new black swimsuit for the holiday, as her old one was starting to fade. Gabby had changed into a yellow swimsuit to match her sundress. *Good grief, that girl's co-ordinated. At least she's not wearing one of her tiny bikinis. They make me feel so inadequate.* As she sat she tugged her sweatshirt over her lap to hide her stomach.

Clare screwed up her eyes against the sun to watch the cousins playing in the shallows. Those not in the boat were bodyboarding. Sally looked as though she was doing more talking than surfing, making a half-hearted attempt to catch the occasional wave. Sophie was wearing a plastic bag over the cut on her foot to protect it from the sea and sand so she was unable to surf. She was notionally in charge of Pepper, but ignored him as he jumped the waves trying to join everyone on the boards or in the boat. She had her phone with her and was taking photos and videos of all the action.

Clare could see that Sal, standing next to Sophie and Ellen, had a heavier build than her cousins. Lisa's two were both tall and willowy like their mother, whereas Sally was of average weight. *Oh well*, she had to concede, *taking after their mothers!* Satisfied to have her in sight, Clare then scanned the beach for Holly who was bobbing up and down in the inflatable boat with Toby. She was similar to Sally in build, although her hair was fairer. *That'll probably darken to the same dreary shade as mine in a few years*, thought Clare wistfully, lying back down to read her book. She soon lost herself in the story – a third murder was just being described in rather too much detail for her liking.

As the sun rose in the sky, the adults lazed on their rugs in the shelter of the dunes and enjoyed doing as little as possible. Eventually, Gabby joined Sam for a paddle in the shallows, where he was standing admiring his choice of present for Toby, and watching the children splashing about. Sam was in his element, enjoying the great outdoors. He had always been athletic, and although he didn't do much organised sport since his move to the city, he was a member of a gym and was a frequent visitor there. He also went running in the rare lunch hours he took, pounding the London pavements. He was proud of his physique, and planned to keep in good shape as he got older. *Unlike Nick*, he told himself, who was starting to thicken at the waist. *Use it or lose it,* was Sam's mantra. He was wondering whether to get into his trunks and go for a swim, or have a beer. *Hmm... beer or swim? Tough call!*

"Well, that boat was a success," he said smugly to Gabby as she strolled up and interrupted his decision-making.

"Great fun!" agreed Gabby.

He folded his arms around her waist as he watched the children enjoy his treat, and rested his chin on her right shoulder. She smelt of her usual heady French perfume. He nuzzled his nose into her hair, breathing in her scent. Gabby had added an acid-yellow visor to her ensemble to protect her hair. The wind had got up, and there was now a stiff breeze, but with the hot sun, it didn't feel cold.

She turned to gaze up at him, thinking what a good uncle he was being. He planted a kiss on her nose. *He would make a wonderful father,* she thought.

Toby and Holly had been abandoned by the others, and were playing with the boat on their own. Sal and Ellen had taken their body boards to catch the surf, and were being watched by Sophie and Pepper. As they stood at the water's edge, Lisa picked her way down from the barbeque site and dragged Sophie away from the water's edge, worrying about her wound getting wet. As Sam and Gabby gazed out at the vista, Holly leapt out of the boat to tell Lisa all about it, leaving Toby on his own with the boat and the oars.

Toby had rowed away further down the beach but eventually decided to bring the boat back in to land. It was more fun being with someone else to boss around, and Holly was still talking to Lisa and Sophie. As always, he was feeling hungry, so decided to make sure his father was getting the barbeque on the go.

He climbed out of his new prized possession and started to remove the oars. In the process he didn't notice that he had dropped the rope attached to the boat. The tide had now turned to go out and the fast current was pulling the boat away from him. The rope disappeared under the surf. Sam was watching Toby struggling with the oars and noticed the rope floating in the water. He shouted out to him.

"Don't let the boat go, Toby! Catch the rope!"

The wind snatched his words, so Toby couldn't hear him. Sam let go of Gabby, ordering, "Watch my trainers!" and walked towards Toby to help. He shouted again.

"Catch the rope, Toby!"

Toby saw Sam approaching and waving wildly to him, but again the wind whipped his words away. Toby turned around to look at the boat. It was only then that he realised the tide had turned and was taking the boat away from him, along with its rope. He stood holding his oars, wondering what to do with them. He couldn't put them down in case they floated away. Like his father, he was not a quick thinker in a crisis.

Sam had now reached his side, and was standing by Toby in the shallows. He was still fully clothed, but he started to turn up the bottoms of his expensive chinos as he realised Toby was dithering.

"Look, pass me the oars, then go and get the boat!" ordered Sam, but as he spoke he could see the boat was still drifting away into deeper water.

Christ! I might as well get the bloody thing myself, he thought as he strode out a few paces. Just as he got within a hand's reach of the boat a gust of wind caught it and turned it over, away from the beach.

Nick now joined Gabby down at the water's edge, from where he had been considering lighting the barbeque. He realised that the boat was in danger of blowing away without the weight of a crew member sitting in it as ballast. Standing at the surf's edge, and also dressed in expensive jeans and trainers, he wasn't able to be of much use. *No point us both getting wet*, he thought to himself, so he stayed on the dry sand. Sam looked at him chatting to Gabby in his dry clothes, and guessed what Nick was thinking. His eyes narrowed. He looked to see where Sally was, but she was hunting for surfing waves to ride, oblivious to anything else.

Sam took another two paces towards the boat. He was now wet up to his knees. His chinos were soaked, but the boat was tantalisingly close. He almost got his hand on it again, when a second gust flipped the boat over once more, sending it another few metres further out from dry land. Sam now had an audience, with nobody doing anything to help.

Nick was standing with Toby, reassuring him that his uncle would rescue his beloved new present. Toby stood with a long face, hoping that his father was right. He wanted to cry, but he felt that he couldn't do that, not now he was thirteen. *At least I held onto my oars*, he consoled himself.

Sam was now frozen to the spot with indecision, furious with Toby for letting the boat go, frustrated at the thought of losing such an expensive purchase on its first outing. *Bloody hell!* He had been planning to take Gabby for a little row later to show off his skills.

By now his soaked trousers were uncomfortable and sticking to his legs. He didn't want to go in any deeper but the boat was again within reach. Clare and Lisa had joined the small group of onlookers, and began to giggle at Sam's dilemma; it was the expression on his face. He could see Gabby looking concerned, but his sisters... *Are they actually fucking laughing at me? Unbelievable!*

Sam's macho nature suddenly kicked in, and he determined to save the boat, come what may. *Bugger the clothes.* He waded towards the boat, now up to his thighs in water. He reached out, and his fingers were centimetres from the rope when a third gust took the boat out of his reach, flipping it over and over, out to sea. It quickly became a yellow spot on the navy blue water.

Sam was speechless with fury. He was fully clothed,

soaked almost to his waist, and for nothing. Just as he turned around to give up and head for shore, a big wave caught him and he lost his balance, tumbling into the surf.

As he emerged from the water, he heard gales of laughter from nearby. He shook the salt water from his eyes to see a crowd enjoying his misfortune. He swore loudly as he strode back, ahead of the others, to the picnic spot, and grabbed a beach towel. The others slowly joined him.

"Well, you lot were a great help!" he snarled at them as they joined him in the picnic area.

He tried to peel off his jeans under a huge beach towel. Gabby made a move to help, but he warded her off. "I can manage, thanks," he stormed, but as soon as the words were out of his mouth he lost his balance a second time, falling over with his trousers around his ankles. His loving sisters, Clare and Lisa, turned away, almost crying with laughter but they tried hard to hide their hilarity from him. Only then did he notice something in Clare's hand – her phone.

"Please, don't tell me you were taking photos," he thundered, the towel now wrapped round his waist. Clare's face was pink with laughter.

"Instead of trying to help save your son's boat, you just stood there taking photos? Well, of all the…" Words failed him.

"Oh, Sam, you should have seen your face. You stood there, not knowing whether to go forwards or back… and when you fell over, well…" Clare rocked with laughter, tears running down her cheeks.

Sam swore, and the rest of the adults realised that he was going to need to be nursed back to good humour. He liked few things less than being teased by his big sisters. Gabby had not seen Sam's bad temper before now, but the others had. They knew he wouldn't calm down for several hours.

Nick handed him a can of beer. "Well done for

trying," he said in a reassuring voice, attempting to improve Sam's mood. Sam was having none of it. Nick should have helped instead of standing in the dry. He took the beer in silence.

"Actually, I wasn't taking photos," explained Clare. "It was a video. I tell you what," she continued, in an attempt to cajole him into a better mood, "I'll send this to *You've Been Framed*, and if it wins we'll buy Toby a new boat, and you can have the rest of the money for some new jeans. How's that?"

Sam glared at her. *So, not only have I wasted money on that boat, I am also going to be made a fool of on prime-time TV! Fan-fucking-tastic!*

"I'll get the barbeque on," said Nick quickly, in an attempt to improve the atmosphere, which had suddenly become frostier than the beers in the cool box.

Sam was still working up his bad mood. *No fucking way am I going to let Clare send that video off for everyone in the office to see. I'm going to make sure that it's deleted before the end of the day.*

The children wandered back from the sea. Toby was carrying his useless oars and blaming Holly for the loss of his boat, but she was having none of it. He couldn't even hug Pepper for consolation as the dog was damp and sandy.

"You didn't even want me in the boat, so it was nothing to do with me," Holly kept telling him reasonably, but he wanted someone to blame other than himself.

Sally approached her uncle, unaware of the drop in temperature around him.

"I didn't know that you hadn't brought swimming trunks with you. You should have said – I've got a spare bikini."

With that, she sat down giggling, pleased with her attempt at humour. Sam gave his niece a withering look. Everyone seemed entertained by the incident, other than

Sam – and poor Toby, who had lost his new present. Sam glared at the sand and fussed with it under his feet, his face giving off as much heat as the barbeque.

When Nick eventually shouted that the sausages and burgers were cooked, Sam picked up a burger and walked off to eat alone. Gabby sat wistfully with her arms around her knees, staring out to sea. *Maybe not such a family man after all*, she thought unhappily.

14

King Arthur's Seat

It was the last week of the holiday. Sam and Gabby had returned to London, having enjoyed beautiful weather all weekend. The only storm clouds had been Sam's – over the fiasco with Toby's boat. He had eventually regained his good humour, but not until the following day. The only person who had taken any notice of his black mood was Gabby, who had tried to speak to him once they were alone. Although, she soon realised that leaving him to cool down in his own time was the easiest option. She eventually gave up trying to cajole him, and put on her headphones to zone him out.

Today, the family in Bay View Cottage was off to visit Enid in Penclawdd. Lisa and the girls had been over earlier in the week, so Clare felt that it was her turn to see her mother. Everyone was going from Bay View Cottage, except for Nick. As the family sat, planning the day over breakfast, he made his excuses.

"Sorry, darling," he grimaced, turning to Clare. "I'll have to dip out. I've got a report to write, and Tom has asked me to take part in a conference call."

"Oh, you poor thing," grumbled Clare on his behalf. "It's not much of a holiday when you have to do things like that. You may as well be in work."

"Well, three weeks is a long time to be away. I did warn you. Don't you worry about me," he reassured her. "Tell you what – leave Pepper with me and I'll take him for a long walk later. I'll enjoy the break after all the office work."

"You are such a sweetheart," smiled Clare. "You

know he always feels cooped up at Mum's, with all her furniture and bric-a-brac to watch out for."

Nick smiled, pleased to have escaped a family visit, and for getting brownie points to boot. The reality was that Nick had an ulterior motive. It turned out that Pepper's cuteness was rather good for pulling the ladies. A drink at one of the local hostelries later on, with him in tow, might hopefully prove interesting. He had just started to read Keith Richards' autobiography, *Life,* and was really enjoying it. *Now there's a guy that lives life to the max. Calls women 'bitches', and his mates 'cats', like some beatnik throwback, but does exactly what he wants. Lucky bastard! I need to take a leaf out of his book.*

"You all go off and enjoy yourselves for the day," encouraged Nick, "and don't worry about me. Make sure you pass my regards on to your mother."

Clare drove off with the children, leaving Nick to text Annabelle to arrange a video chat during her lunch hour. He really fancied doing a 'Dirty Den' and exposing himself to her online to remind her of what she was missing. He decided against it, realising that it might take some explaining if a colleague walked in on him and saw his member on Annabelle's screen.

He cast his mind back to the newspaper headlines when the scandal broke. *Now... what was his name... it wasn't Dirty Den. Got it! Lesley Grantham. He must have been bloody mortified when it all hit the papers – a well-known celebrity having a wank in front of a stranger. Why would you jeopardise your career like that? Funny old world!*

Instead, he considered placing the computer on the kitchen table and taking matters in hand underneath it while he was talking to her. *Yeah, that's safe enough. Maybe get her to expose some of her luscious tits for a mo – no, too risky.* Just the thought of what was to come was making him horny. He unzipped his flies.

* * *

Across the other side of the Gower, Clare and the children piled into Enid's tiny, two-up, two-down Victorian terraced cottage. There was a neat front room facing the road that was hardly ever used, especially since Enid's husband, Howard, had died.

The back living room had been knocked through into the kitchen, making one large kitchen and seating area facing a wood-burner, where Enid spend most of her time when she was at home. The kitchen also held a sky blue *Aga* on the far wall, so the room was always cosy in winter. During those few weeks of summer when the temperature slowly climbed up the thermometer, Enid turned the *Aga* off and lived off salads and microwave snacks. That was, until autumn chills nudged her into switching the range back on again for the cold, damp, winter months.

The stable door opened onto a quaint courtyard that ended in a low, thick, sea wall. There were solid benches for sitting on and enjoying the sea views beyond the wall. On the far side, was a three-metre drop down to sea level. These days the sea had receded half a mile, allowing salt marshes to take hold. Local farmers made use of this habitat by grazing sheep there. Salt marsh lamb was a local delicacy, along with samphire; known as 'poor man's asparagus'.

Enid switched the kettle on, and heard all about the drama of the lost boat for the second time. Lisa and her girls had told her their version of events when they had visited. She didn't mind. It was a good story, although Toby still had to accept that nobody was planning to replace the boat as he had hoped. Once the tea was made, and she had caught up with all the gossip, she told the children that she had something to shown them in the front room. They all wandered into the formal little room. On the table in the centre were some old tins laid out.

"I've been sorting out your grandfather's photos," Enid explained to the children, "and I found these from when he was in the army during the Second World War."

The children started to look through the small black and white photographs, showing soldiers in a variety of off-duty poses.

"He was a Desert Rat, you know," she proudly reminded the children.

"What was that?" asked Toby.

"It means that he fought with a famous tank regiment in North Africa. Then he went to Italy, but got injured and had to return home to Wales." Enid smiled fondly as she remembered her much-missed husband.

She picked one of the photos up and handed it around. "Look, here he is sitting on one of the tanks he used to drive."

"Cool!" muttered Toby, wishing he could have a go at driving a tank. The nearest he got to modern warfare was playing *Call of Duty* at his friend's house. He had to sneak round there to play it as his mother had said he was too young.

"They're very hot, actually, from what I gathered," corrected Enid, taking her grandson's comment literally.

Clare suggested "There's a company in Abingdon that can put photos onto a disc, so you can store them on your computer. Would you like me to take them and have that done, Mum? We could have copies too. And I'm sure Sam and Lisa would also like some."

"Oh, would you do that, dear? That would be lovely! Look, here are some of when he was a boy."

And so the morning passed; looking at old photos and reminiscing about an old soldier. After lunch, they climbed into their cars and drove to the middle of the Gower to park near Arthur's Seat, a Neolithic burial chamber at Cefn Bryn.

As they clambered up the bracken-covered hill to the historical site, Clare suggested that King Arthur must have been one of Britain's first tourists, as he allegedly visited Glastonbury, Tintagel, and numerous other sites. Their reward for the climb was panoramic views of both the north and south coasts of the peninsular.

As they stood admiring the stones, Enid told the children some of the legends about the site, as if the children were hearing them for the first time.

After their return walk they crossed the quiet road to the *King Arthur* for reviving drinks, sitting in the early evening sun in the large busy beer garden.

Enid eventually said her goodbyes and returned home to Penclawdd and a scheduled game of bowls. Clare drove the children back to Mumbles, still talking about their grandfather and his photographs. She was looking forward to showing Nick the old photos of her father. He had always got on so well with Howard. She felt so sorry at the thought of Nick missing out on such a lovely day. *Poor thing!*

Nick, meanwhile, had had a wonderful day. He had enjoyed the steamy video call with Annie that he had planned then, following a quick dog walk, had met up with Nia, who was staying in the apartments behind the *Langland Brasserie*. Pepper had been left in the car in the shade of a large oak tree for the afternoon while Nick and Nia had energetic sex in the king-sized bed in the master bedroom of Nia's apartment. Nick could trust Pepper not to tell tales.

15

The Dog Day

The end of the holidays was fast approaching. The three weeks had not been without incident, but overall it had been a success. *Only one or two days of rain, an argument on the drive, a cut foot, and a lost boat. Not a bad tally,* thought Clare. *I've had worse holidays.*

Sam and Gabby had been subdued following the loss of Toby's boat. Gabby had been upset at the bad mood and rudeness shown by Sam, and their entire weekend had been overshadowed by his poor attitude. Their spoiled holiday break had been unfortunate, but Clare was sure that they would be back on an even keel by now. She would wait until she got home to Abingdon, before she checked with Sam to see how things were between the two of them. *Anyway,* Clare thought, *Gabby has to find out at some time about Sam's temper. He's always been the same. Typical alpha male!*

Lisa, on the other hand, had been twitching to go home since Phil had announced his departure the previous week. Even more so, since Sophie had cut her foot the day after he left, and he'd taken the family car. Lisa had thought that he would return in a day or two, which is why she had allowed him to take the car. But once he'd started work, he'd been offered more gigs at a higher rate of pay than usual. He had phoned and discussed the situation with Lisa.

"I'll come back if you really want me to, but to be honest these guys are great. They really like my stuff, and they want to work on producing some of my songs. I think I might get a break with them."

Lisa had been torn. She wanted him to be with her to help out with the girls but, if the money was that good, it would make sense for him to stay where he was. In the end she relented, and agreed that he should stay put. She had suggested to the children that they go home early, but Ellen had made such a fuss that Lisa had given up trying to cut short the holiday, and resigned herself to the full three weeks. As far as she was concerned, their return home couldn't come soon enough. In future, she would book two weeks max.

* * *

It had rained earlier in the day and, although the showers had now stopped, there was still a stiff breeze. This was their last evening, and Toby called in to ask his cousins if they wanted to go for one last trip to Rhossili Bay before supper. Ellen leapt up to go, but Sophie decided to stay curled up with her book.

Nick had been the one to initiate the idea, and had offered to take the kids to Rhossili Bay beach again, despite it being the scene of the lost boat.

"Are you sure you want to go all that way?" Clare had asked him. "The kids seem happy enough, and it might rain again. Plus, we still haven't finished the packing."

"Oh, stop fussing!" he snapped. "The dog needs a run, and I fancy one last walk on the beach before we head home tomorrow. The kids have been cooped up all afternoon with the rain. We might as well take advantage of the fact that it's stopped at last."

In reality, Nick was feeling claustrophobic; he was the one wanting to get out. The vast expanse of wild, unspoiled beach was calling him. It would be months before he would have the chance to hear the sound of the sea again.

Clare shrugged. She was happy to have some space to carry on packing, and tidy up the cottage. *Typical Nick, giving me a break from the kids so I can get on with what needs doing.*

Nick loaded the car with their three children, cousin Ellen, and Pepper, leaving Clare to prepare an easy supper of lasagne and salad for everyone. Lisa had offered to bring round a pudding and some garlic bread. Enid was coming over later to say goodbye and bring some Welsh cakes for them to take home to England. Nobody had the heart to tell her that they could buy them in Abingdon in their local supermarket.

* * *

Nick drove in silence across the moor that divided the two sides of the Gower, ignoring the wild Welsh ponies that were standing around glumly like underpaid film extras. He drove into the car park. It was almost empty, situated in the shelter of the high sand dunes that hid the huge, sweeping bay on the far side. As they all climbed out of the car, Nick ordered the children to leave their phones behind.

"You don't want them being dropped in the sea," he reminded them.

They dutifully switched them off and hid them in various nooks in the car, then ran over the dunes after Pepper to the water's edge. There weren't many people about. The earlier rain had sent the day-trippers home in a sulk. There was a small number of hardier surfers on the choppy waves further down the beach, braving the gusting winds in wetsuits. The lifeguards had long since packed up. The tide was just starting to go out, leaving a swathe of flat, damp sand. One or two of the braver gulls were playing kamikaze on the high winds, shrieking calls to each other as they swooped overhead.

Nick clambered over the dunes for long enough to check that the children were in his sight. Then he sat in a dip near the top of the dunes to avoid the worst of the wind. He took his phone out of his pocket, pressed a familiar name on speed-dial, and settled down for a long chat.

In the distance the children were having a fine time.

They were standing just out of the water's reach, throwing a tennis ball into the sea for Pepper to fetch and bring back. It was a game that Pepper never tired of playing.

Sally, however, soon got bored and strolled towards the stumpy wooden remains of the old ship, *Helvetia,* at the far end of the beach. It sat exposed on the sand at low tide, like the upturned ribcage of a whale. Sally was imagining the crew that might have lost their lives during the shipwreck, her vivid imagination inventing dramatic scenarios. Low, grey clouds were scudding overhead, adding to the drama. It looked like rain was approaching again.

Toby and Ellen were having a competition to see who could throw the ball the farthest. Pepper thought that this was a great game, as he could then have more time swimming, even though his legs were beginning to tire. Holly felt ignored by the two older children, and demanded her turn at throwing the ball.

"Shut up, Squirt," said Toby. "You can't throw it far enough."

"I can, just you watch! I'm in the school rounder's team, for your information," retorted Holly.

Toby relented and tossed the ball to Holly. She was wearing her waterproof shoes, so she ran out into the shallow water, calling for Pepper to follow her.

"That's cheating!" shouted Toby, laughing at the antics of the two of them.

As she waded into the water with the dog following, big heavy drops of rain started to fall on their faces. The two without the ball turned to head back to the car, leaving Holly to follow with Pepper. Pepper realised that the game might be ending, and barked for the ball to be thrown again. Holly threw the ball as hard as she could into the waves for the final time and Pepper splashed out to swim after it. Holly turned and waded back towards Toby and Ellen, shouting to them, "See, I told you! Did you see that fantastic throw?"

Pepper had now swum out and claimed the ball, but as he did so, a large wave caught him by surprise. He swallowed seawater and let go of the ball.

Toby turned to insult Holly and looked for Pepper, expecting him to be with her. Instead, he saw that he was still in the sea. The children hadn't been aware of the strong current that was now racing underneath the surface of the sea near the shore. It was dragging the tired little dog further out, despite his frantic doggy-paddling.

The wind was starting to whip the waves higher, creating white horses, and the rain was coming down in squalls.

Toby turned back and called for the cocker spaniel to come back in, but as he looked, Pepper seemed to be drifting away from the shore. Toby shouted his name, but his words were caught by the gusts of wind and lost in mid-air.

The tide was now racing out, and the waves had increased in height, sometimes hiding Pepper. The children realised that Pepper was not responding to Toby's shouts, and was no longer still playing a game. Something was wrong.

"I'm going to swim after him," Toby announced, starting to pull off his trainers. "He must have got caught in one of those currents Mum keeps warning us about."

"Are you sure?" Ellen shouted back in the wind. "What if you get carried out too? Check with Uncle Nick. Remember what happened to the boat."

Holly turned to look for her father, who she could just about see in the distance, sitting on the dunes with his phone. She waved her arms at him.

"Dad! Dad, come and help Pepper! He can't get in," she yelled. But he was too far away to hear her.

Toby and Ellen also started waving and shouting and Nick gradually realised that they wanted him and were not just waving for fun. He impatiently ended his phone call to respond to the children.

Only now did he notice that it was raining. The dunes had given him some shelter, and he was wearing his waterproof jacket, so he hadn't noticed.

He noted that the dog was not with them. *Where the hell's he got to?* He started to jog towards the children as Holly ran towards him. She was close enough now for him to see that she was crying.

"Dad, we need you. Pepper can't get back in," she cried.

He put his arm around her shoulders to reassure her, and they both started jogging towards Ellen and Toby. The pair stood in the shallow water, shouting at the waves. Sally was striding back from her solitary walk, the rain and wind driving her towards them.

"Dad, we've got to go after Pepper. He can't get back in," shouted Toby frantically.

"You're *not* going in there," stated Nick firmly. He had to shout over the sound of the surf. "And that's final! If the currents are strong enough to carry the dog, they'll take you. Let's just think for a second."

He wondered what the hell he was going to do. He had seen enough news stories about people losing their lives trying to rescue their dogs from lakes, rivers, and surf to know that it wasn't a good idea. He had no intention of making the front page of tomorrow's *South Wales Echo*.

At a loss, he looked around to see if any surfers were still in the water. But, as it was early evening and now raining heavily, most of them had left the beach. *Anyway, would they be able to lift a dog onto their boards and still get back to shore? And where are the bloody lifeguards when you want them?* He looked around for help but there was nobody in sight. At this time of day the lifeguards were long gone.

The seas looked threatening under the black clouds and frighteningly powerful. There were not usually many boats in this bay as the tides were too strong for them to anchor. *What the hell shall I do? I need to phone Clare.* He went to grab his phone from his pocket but it wasn't there. *Shit! It must have dropped out of my pocket when I stood up.*

"For Christ's sake! I'll have to go back to the dunes to find my phone," he bellowed to the children. "Come on!" he ordered and turned to march away. The children didn't follow.

"We can't leave Pepper," howled Holly. Nick stood there in a quandary. *What the hell shall I do? It's like the damned boat all over again.* As he floundered, Sally appeared beside him.

He turned to her. "Thank Christ you're back," he said to her. "Stay here with the others while I make a phone call, but don't let anyone into the water, whatever happens."

Nick left them by the pounding waves to return to the dunes to search for his phone. He found it exactly where he had been sitting, and phoned Clare. When she answered his call, he didn't know what to say. His head was pounding with tension, just like the waves on the beach.

"Hi, I thought you'd be back by now," Clare said brightly. "Mum's here and the lasagne is in the oven. Are you on the way back?"

"No. We've lost the dog…" Nick quickly explained what had happened, ending with, "I don't know what to do, and the children don't want to leave."

"Oh no!" exclaimed Clare. "Hang on, I'll speak to Mum." She had a quick word with her mother to update her and agree on a decision.

"Mum said you should phone 999 for the coastguard and see what they advise. Once you've done that, and heard what they say, bring the children back for supper, then we'll all walk down to the Lifeboat Station. It's only ten minutes from the cottage. If the children know they can go there later, they won't mind leaving the beach."

Of course! The Lifeboat Station was at the end of the

Mumbles Promenade, beyond the pier. Nick, relieved to have the decisions made for him, ended the call, saying they would be back in half an hour or so. He jogged back to the water's edge. There was now no sign of the little black cocker spaniel. The kids told Nick that Pepper had not been since he had left them. He had hoped that this was all a bad dream and the dog would have magically reappeared.

"I'm going to phone the coastguard and see what they can do," he informed the children.

By now, all four children were crying. His hands were shaking as he pressed 999, only to find that there was no signal at the water's edge. *Fuck! He should have stayed on the dunes, not come back down to speak to the kids.*

As he turned to head back to the dunes, an elderly couple approached in wet weather gear, suspecting that something was amiss. Nick briefly explained what was happening and asked them to watch the children. He still worried that Toby might be tempted to swim out, despite the uninviting surf.

"Oh, the poor little doggy," exclaimed the lady. "Will he be alright?"

Well, obviously fucking not, thought Nick viciously, but instead of ranting, he turned and strode off without bothering to reply. He was getting a headache. As soon as he reached the higher peak of the dunes, his phone regained a signal, and he pressed 999 again.

"Hello, Emergency Services. Which service do you require?" asked a calm, pleasant voice. Nick asked for the coastguard and almost cried with frustration as he was asked for his personal details, slowing down his connection. When he was eventually put through, he explained the situation.

"Can you still see the dog, sir?" he was asked.

"Not from here," replied Nick, "But the children are still on the beach looking for him. They were throwing a ball for him, you see…" His voice trailed off.

"I see, sir," said the voice with a perceptible sigh, suggesting that the public never learned. Nick imagined the employee shaking his head.

"Well, we could get the inshore rib out, but by the time it launches from Mumbles and gets around Worms Head that will be another half an hour…"

It was his turn to leave the sentence unfinished. His tone of voice suggested that the call out would be a waste of time. It was now around 7 pm and it would only get darker. Pepper was black. The situation was all too quickly descending into a nightmare for Nick. What could he say?

"Oh, that would be fantastic," pleaded Nick. "The children won't leave the beach without him."

"Very well, sir. We'll bring the launch around to Rhossili Bay. We'll have your number, so we'll call and let you know the outcome of our search. Please try to stay away from the beach. There's nothing you can do there. I advise you in the strongest possible terms *not* to let the children enter the water. We don't want any further problems."

With that, he rang off, leaving Nick looking at the waves in despair. *Now what? Nothing for it but to walk back down to the water to collect the bloody kids.*

By the time he reached them, the rain had passed overhead to soak another beach. A small group of onlookers had gathered, waiting to hear the results of Nick's call. He explained that the coastguard was coming out from Mumbles to look for Pepper. *My, don't people enjoy a drama*, he thought bitterly.

The children were wet, red-eyed, and tear-stained. Nick felt like crying himself, not for the dog, but in self-pity at having to deal with such a crap situation. Again, he didn't know what to do. Should he head back to the cottage, or stay on the beach? The coastguard had his number, and had said they couldn't do anything to help. He squatted down in front of the children and explained that the coastguard was coming out, trying to keep the frustration out of his voice. He managed to thank the elderly couple for staying with the children all this time, and made to walk back to the car, but Holly blocked his path.

"We can't go, Dad. Pepper will be looking for us," she wailed.

"There's no point staying here. We might as well head back to the cottage for supper..." he started. This was met by such howls of protest from the children that he realised he would get nowhere with this idea.

Nick looked down at Holly's pitiful face. He couldn't bear to tell her his thoughts that by now Pepper must surely have drowned, so he said nothing. At that moment, Toby shouted that the lifeboat was approaching, so Nick knew that the children would now definitely want to stay and watch the rescue attempt.

The morose group stood on the shore, watching as the boat started to work in a zig-zag out to where Nick had said the dog might have drifted.

After an hour the boat turned and headed back towards the headland with no indication to those watching on the beach that they had picked up an additional passenger. The group trudged back to the car in silence, apart from Holly's wailing. Once in the car, Nick handed his phone to Sally.

"Phone your mum and let her know we're on our way back," he said tersely.

Sally did so, giving those in the cottage an update of the situation. As they returned across the bleak moor, the children started to come up with all the ways in which Pepper might be saved: the lifeboat had actually picked him up but they hadn't noticed; he was picked up by a passing boat; he had swum to shore further down the beach; he was picked up by a surfer; and so on. The alternative was too dreadful to imagine.

By the time they got back to the cottage they had almost convinced themselves that Pepper was tucking into his biscuits somewhere, safe and dry. But the minute they walked into the kitchen and saw his abandoned dinner bowl on the floor, their optimism evaporated. Holly ran crying into Clare's arms to tell her all about the drama.

Enid took over in the kitchen, and started to serve up platefuls of lasagne, salad, and garlic bread. No-one had much of an appetite, apart from Nick who was ravenous after all his running up and down the beach. The incident hadn't dented his appetite, and he washed the food down with several glasses of red wine to try and unwind. Once they had all eaten, Enid shooed them out.

"Off you go," she commanded. "Walk down to the Lifeboat Station to find out if there's any news! I'll wash up here." She was glad to be alone and of some use. She couldn't bear to see her grandchildren looking so upset.

They all trudged out into the damp night air to walk down to the Lifeboat Station, gratefully leaving the clearing up to Enid. They reached there just as the crew was finishing washing the salt water off the boat that had been out on the search. They confirmed that they hadn't seen the dog and – out of the hearing of the children – mused that he would most definitely have been washed out to sea in the strong undercurrents in the present tidal conditions.

In a desperate bid to retrieve something from the awful evening, Clare suggested a final stop in *Verdi's* for one last treat of coffee and cake or ice cream. Despite her prompts, there were no takers, so they headed back to Bay View Cottage.

Lisa and her girls said goodnight and wended their way home, with Lisa explaining that this was one of the reasons that they couldn't own a dog. Then Enid left, promising to return the following morning to see if there was any news. With lots of hugs and kisses, she left the family to their miserable last evening in the cottage.

16

The Aftermath

Sally took her younger brother and sister upstairs to help them to get ready for bed before Clare went up to settle them down for the night.

The minute they were alone, Clare turned to Nick who was sitting at the dining table, opening another bottle of red wine.

"Where were you when it all happened? Clare demanded. "You weren't with them."

Nick had his back to her. "On the phone," he stated flatly.

"Who to?" There was a long, heavy pause. Nick's head was pounding with the tension of the accident and too much red wine.

"Annabelle... about work." As soon as the words came out he realised his mistake.

"Annabelle? Your secretary? On a Friday night? On the beach? What was so urgent that you needed to phone her on a Friday night?" queried Clare, puzzled. He paused again, unprepared for the questioning.

"Oh, something about a meeting on Monday morning... she needed some information for it. Don't forget, I've been out of the office for three weeks," he pointed out.

As far as he was concerned that was the matter finished. He turned and walked out of the room, making his escape. Clare watched him as he walked into the kitchen, and suddenly she *knew.*

Just a split-second's pause was all he had taken to reply, but she recognised his every nuance after twenty years of marriage. She had always trusted Nick implicitly and never doubted his fidelity... until now. All of a sudden she guessed that he and Annabelle must be having an affair. He was always so honest and open with her, but the way he had acted had been out of character. The turned back, and the pause before answering, as if he had something to hide.

She slumped onto the nearest chair and stared into space, unable to deal with what she had just discovered – or thought that she had discovered. *I'm over-reacting because of Pepper*, she tried to convince herself. But it was true. She was certain.

After a few minutes that seemed like hours, Clare stood up and followed Nick into the kitchen.

"What did Annabelle need to know about the meeting on Monday?" she asked him quietly.

Nick was standing at the sink, looking out of the window, even though it was black outside and there was nothing to see. He had thought that the conversation had ended, and was again taken by surprise. It was unlike Clare to question him like this. He had lied to her so often over the years that it was second nature, but his lies went unchallenged. This was different.

"Oh, you know... the usual... she just wanted to run something by me... checking some figures..." he said, being as casual and careful as he could.

Damn. Why didn't I say I was talking to Tom? Oh, well, *too late now.*

"So you said," snapped Clare, "but what in particular? What figures would she want to run by you on a Friday night?"

He faltered at the tone of her voice. "Nothing important... I told you..." he stammered.

He was so frazzled after the surreal evening that this just seemed an extension of a bad dream. Clare had never quizzed him before, and he had not thought to prepare a cover story. After nearly twenty years of marriage, he had become totally used to Clare believing anything he told her without question. *Honest to God, wasn't it bad enough having to deal with all that crap at the beach without this now? Give me a break!* He really didn't feel up to an interrogation.

Clare stared at him in amazement. He was so obviously lying, and doing it so badly. *How dare he? Couldn't he even give her the respect she deserved, and make up some fantastic inventive lie to bamboozle her?* She grabbed the back of a chair to steady herself. She wanted to stop but she couldn't. She needed to know the truth, however painful. She forced herself to continue, to confront him.

"You're lying," she stated flatly. It was a statement, not a question.

She noticed that Nick's neck went a pale pink as he blushed. She hadn't realised that the back of a neck could blush.

"Don't be ridiculous. Why would I lie?" he blustered, but he still didn't turn around to face her. He started to load the dishwasher, looking for a diversion.

"Exactly! Why would you lie?" she repeated bleakly. "There's only one reason, isn't there?"

The question hung in the air between them, with neither of them wanting to break the silence. At that precise moment, Holly walked into the kitchen in tears, oblivious to the frigid atmosphere.

"It's all my fault that Pepper got…" She choked on her words. "If I hadn't thrown that ball so hard…" She tried to continue but her body was racked by sobs.

With a look of relief on his face at being given a diversion, Nick swept Holly into his arms and headed for her bedroom to try and settle her to sleep. It was Clare's turn to gaze out of the kitchen window at nothing. Her reflection stared grimly back at her.

Holly's interruption could not have come at a worse time for Clare. She had wanted the truth, but didn't think she had heard it. Holly's arrival reminded Clare of her responsibilities to the children. *God! The children! How could I possibly tear them away from their father?* She had to stop herself from crying like Holly. *Hang on, hang on, get a grip... you don't even know for sure...* But she definitely did.

She walked over to the kettle, needing a cup of tea. As the kettle boiled, she pondered over the interrupted conversation. Did she really want to confront him and force him to reveal something that might change their relationship forever?

By the time Nick returned from reassuring Holly that she wasn't to blame for Pepper's disappearance, half an hour had passed. The time with Holly had given him enough of a break to pull himself together. He went to the table and picked up his refilled glass of wine, then came and sat next to Clare on the sofa. He put his arm around her shoulders.

"Now, you silly goose, don't be having any ideas about anything happening between me and Annabelle. You've seen her – she's got thighs like tree trunks – not my type at all." He gave her a kiss on the cheek. "You know there's no-one for me except you, don't you?" he continued. "Always has been."

He gave her what he hoped was a winning smile. Then he grabbed the TV remote, turning away from Clare in the process. As far as he was concerned, the whole episode could now be forgotten. *Normal service has been resumed. After all, it was only a bloody phone call when all's said and done.*

Clare sat next to Nick – the person she thought she knew best in the world – and didn't know what to think. Had their entire marriage just been smoke and mirrors? Would he – could he – be unfaithful to her? She hoped not.

He was right about one thing, though. Clare had met Annabelle, and she did have huge thighs, but she was also quite voluptuous, with a generous bosom that was always on show. She was also very pretty and much younger than Clare. In fact, thinking about it, she didn't know anyone who had a secretary older than their wife. *How was that?*

The longer she sat on the sofa next to him, oblivious of what he was watching on TV, the more she tried to convince herself that she must have been mistaken.

17

Return Journey

Early next morning Nick was at the wheel of the car, delighted to be heading back home over the bridge to England. He felt that the drama over the dog had diverted Clare's attention from that brief blip last night when she had accused him of an affair with Annabelle. *That had been close!* He couldn't make out what had come over Clare. She was usually such a trusting puss.

He re-ran the events of the previous evening in his mind yet again to make sure that he had covered his tracks. She never touched his mobile, but even so he had gone through his phone log late last night while she was asleep, deleting Annabelle's texts and call logs.

Nick had read too many stories about blokes being caught out by their mobile phones or emails, although he had never felt the need to worry about them himself – until now. Modern technology was certainly a double-edged sword.

He remembered Ben, a colleague in the London office, who had carried on an affair quite happily for over three years with a girl in HR. Then, one night, out of the blue, his wife picked up his phone and read a steamy text from the mistress. What had possessed his wife to act, Ben never discovered. He was booted out of his much-loved family home and the locks to his front door were changed by the enraged wife before he could turn round. The divorce was finalised in weeks, and he was now married to the girlfriend, living in a pokey semi with two toddlers whose names he could only just about remember. Ben often spoke wistfully about his first wife, who was still living in their substantial detached villa with their two adorable teenagers. She refused to forgive him, never mind speak to him.

As Nick drove, his thoughts rambled back to the time when Prince Charles' phone call to Camilla was taped and printed in the trash press. He had still been married to Princess Diana at the time, and the conversation was full of explicit sexual references. At least that particular trap wouldn't happen to him. *Christ, all that talk about tampons. Charlie must have died of embarrassment. There's a downside to being famous…*

His daydream was interrupted by Toby tapping his shoulder. "Can we phone Granny again to see if the coastguard has any news?"

Nick took a moment to remember what the 'news' might be before he shook his head.

"We'll phone when we get home, but don't build your hopes up."

Clare looked over at him and frowned. *He could try and sound more sympathetic,* she thought sourly.

The children were very subdued. Holly had cried all through breakfast and was still saying it was her fault that Pepper drowned – if indeed he had. In the end, Toby had turned on her.

"Yes, it was your fault! You're always doing stupid, showing-off stunts." That had set her crying even harder.

"Toby, that wasn't very nice. You like to show off, too!" snapped Clare.

Toby had looked up in surprise. His mother rarely told him off. He had gone upstairs and thrown himself on his bed to sulk in comfort, until she had called him down to walk to the Lifeboat Station. Enid had called in after breakfast to say goodbye to everyone, and they had all walked along to the Lifeboat Station together.

Nobody was on duty to ask about the incident of the previous evening. Clare had phoned the number displayed, and the person on the other end of the phone informed her that there had been no reports of a black cocker spaniel being found. Enid said that she would visit the local police station on her way home to Penclawdd, but that was more to comfort the children than because she thought there was any real chance of finding the missing dog.

As they walked back to the cottage to pack, Clare had tried to lift their sadness, without success.

"What colour would you say the sea is today?" she asked the children. Toby glanced at it and shrugged.

"Dunno. Blue... sort-of."

She laughed as if he had said something witty. "Ooh, I wouldn't say blue, but even if it was, there are lots of shades of blue. What do you think, Holly?"

Holly gazed out beyond the harbour wall over Swansea Bay. "Grey with some bits of brown? Definitely not blue."

Toby glowered at Holly for contradicting him but couldn't be bothered to challenge her. Who cared what colour the sea was, anyway?

"Sal, what would you say?" Clare asked her. Sally had been giving the question serious consideration since her mother had raised the topic, but was struggling to come up with the right colour.

"It's hard to say, because it keeps changing. It does look grey, but then the sun comes out from the clouds and it looks almost yellow. And Holly's right, you can see the brown where the sand gets churned up; so, actually, it's more than one colour."

Sally was pleased with this answer, and got her phone out to take a final holiday snap of the sea. After that the group fell silent again, and trudged back to the cottage to start packing up, each lost in their own thoughts.

Once the car was packed, Clare wandered around the cottage making sure they hadn't left anything behind. Sure enough, there was a t-shirt of Nick's hanging up on a hook behind the bathroom door. As she unhooked it she instinctively buried her face into it to capture his familiar scent. She slumped onto the side of the bath and caught sight of herself in the mirror. *How sad I look*, she thought with surprise. *Is that because of Pepper's accident or because of my suspicions of Nick? Probably both.* She sighed heavily and walked downstairs to re-join her family, pinning a smile on her face in case her mother saw her miserable expression.

The holiday cottage had been such a lovely base for three weeks that, despite the drama of the night before, she felt a pang of regret at leaving Mumbles and returning to everyday life. She looked ruefully at her mother.

"Oh well, time to head back to the real world…"

She gave her mother a big hug and handed her the keys to the cottage. Enid had offered to drop them back to the letting agent anything to make their departure less dreadful.

"I'll phone if I have any news about…" Enid couldn't say the dog's name. Her voice was artificially bright as she tried to sound cheerful, but she was unable to complete her sentence.

She had given herself a pep-talk earlier to make sure she didn't let the grandchildren see her upset but, despite her best efforts, tears pricked at the back of her eyes. Seeing the children so distraught was too sad. No wonder Nick and Clare had hardly said a word to each other since she arrived. *Not surprising, though, considering the drama of the evening before,* she thought. If she had known about the second drama of the evening concerning Nick and Annabelle, she would have wanted to cry even more.

"Got everything?" she asked the topped-up car, before turning away to surreptitiously wipe her eyes. She didn't wait for a reply. "Come on then. Let's get you on the road. Phone me when you get home so I know you got home safely…" her voice faltered.

She waved to the occupants of the car until it drove out of sight. Then, blowing her nose, she briskly locked the cottage door and walked around the corner to say her goodbyes to Lisa's family. Phil had arrived late that morning to take them home. After a second wave of farewells, Enid got into her compact car.

Thank goodness I've got bowls this afternoon to take my mind off this upset, she thought to herself as she drove away from Mumbles.

* * *

As they sped along the M4, Clare sat in the passenger seat in silence, staring woodenly ahead, not wanting to speak. She could hear snatches of conversation from the children in the back.

"He could have swum to shore further down the beach. You know how strong the tides are…"

"He could have lost his way once he swam back to the beach and turned left instead of right…"

"He could have been found and handed in to the RSPCA. We'll have to get in touch with them, too…"

Holly leaned forward towards Clare. "He will be alright, won't he, Mum?" she asked, broken-heartedly.

Clare couldn't bear to tell her what she actually thought. "Maybe, darling. We'll have to wait and see."

Holly continued her conversation with the other two, leaving Clare to sink back to her lonely thoughts. She had lain awake last night with her mind in turmoil, and eventually gone to sleep deciding to abandon her suspicions about Nick and Annabelle. But when she woke at 4 am she had listened to Nick's even breathing, and run back over the last few months since Annabelle had been appointed as Nick's secretary. She tried to recall any changes in Nick's behaviour, but truthfully she could think of nothing.

Last summer had been a strange time. He had been spending a lot of time working late and having to spend more time than usual in London, but he had told her that there was just a load of extra work to do. That was just before his last secretary had left the company, so it was nothing to do with Annabelle.

When Annabelle started working for Nick everything had returned to normal, so Clare couldn't say that Nick had done anything in particular to justify her suspicions. She had only met Annabelle once, and had been secretly pleased to note that she was rather overweight. She didn't know, of course, about the crash diet that had recently transformed Annabelle's figure.

Was she the type to have an affair with a married man who has three children? Clare wondered. Unfortunately, there didn't seem to be a 'type'.

Rain splattered on the windscreen, matching her black mood. Nick turned on the wipers and fiddled with the radio dials, breaking into her depressing train of thought.

"Mind if I put the cricket on, darling?" he asked, placing his hand briefly on her thigh.

"Not at all," she answered, secretly wanting silence in which to brood.

She wanted to scream at him, 'I know you lied to me!', but she didn't know what she would do if she found out the truth. She had never been jealous like she knew Lisa was; she had always thought that it was a wasted emotion that led to problems of its own. *Look what happened to Othello – from love to hate because of a seed of jealousy. Pull yourself together*, she told herself, gazing ahead at the spray being thrown on the windscreen by speeding lorries.

"Everything okay?" asked Nick, giving her what he hoped was a loving smile, and squeezing her leg as if to reassure her that everything was the same as usual.

"Yes, fine," she lied. She didn't return the smile; it wouldn't come.

This is interesting, she mused, *in an affair you would expect that the person hiding the affair would be the liar, not the innocent party. Yet here I am saying that everything's okay. I'm lying through my teeth.*

The car pulled into their drive just over three hours after setting off from the holiday cottage, despite the rain. Clare would usually have teased Nick, and joked about the good time they had made, but she wasn't in the mood for joking.

She eased herself out of the car and collected the leftover-food bags to take into the kitchen to make a scratch lunch. She wanted to go upstairs, close the curtains, shut out the day, and be left alone. Instead, she went through the motions of making food for everyone and laid it out on the kitchen table for the family to help themselves. The kitchen was a reminder of Pepper, with his bowls in the corner waiting to be filled. She quickly stowed them in the dishwasher with the lunch things as she tidied up. The children appeared not to notice and, after eating, went to their rooms to settle back home.

Nick came into the kitchen, having unloaded the car. "I'll pop to the supermarket and get some pizza and salad for supper, shall I? I want to get some beers as well. Do you want anything?"

Clare looked blankly at him, amazed that he was acting so normally. He was as organised as ever. If she could have read his mind she'd have known he desperately wanted to get away and have a talk with Annabelle. But, she couldn't.

"No thanks. Just the usual – bread and milk, and anything else you can think of. I'll do a list later for a proper shop."

How mundane this all is, as if everything is fine between us. She went to the laundry room and started to sort the washing into piles. As she opened the cupboard to lift out the washing-up liquid, she saw the shelf with various dog foods, and her heart sank even lower. She would have to give them away quickly, before the children noticed them. She would give them to Duncan and Debs for little Baxter.

Clare walked over to the window and looked out

onto the back garden. The rain was making rivulets down the glass. A kaleidoscope of colours was visible; her beloved annuals were enjoying soaking up the rain. The colours seemed garish to Clare – she wanted to turn down the volume. They were much too loud. Sepia tones would suit her mood better. *Is this what I want?* She asked herself. *Living a life with a man I no longer trust?*

She was still standing there an hour later, when Nick walked back in laden down with shopping bags. She left him in the kitchen to unpack the food and went to phone her mother.

18

Autumn Leaves

As Clare stood brushing her teeth, she looked at herself critically in the bathroom mirror and thought back over the last few months. This autumn had been the worst time she had ever lived through.

Since they returned from their summer holiday, she had tried to bury her suspicions of that last night. But she soon realised that she needed honesty between herself and Nick to enable her to move forward. For the first time in their relationship, she started to question Nick about his feelings for her. She was suddenly unsure, whereas in the past she had been blissfully content. Following more questioning, Nick had admitted to a 'brief fling that meant nothing' with Annabelle.

If he'd hoped that this course of action would be enough to end the matter, he was right. Clare had forgiven him. She couldn't bear to separate from him and cause the children the inevitable heartache. They were unhappy enough already over the loss of Pepper. After all, for all his faults, Nick was a good father and provider, and the children would probably not understand if she chose not to forgive him for this – in Nick's words – 'meaningless affair'. She had made the hard decision to rise above the affair to keep the marriage together. *And anyway*, she had consoled herself, *what marriage is perfect, after all? It was only the one time in all these years. And he still loves me… and I'm terrified of trying to cope without him.*

* * *

In October, however, Annabelle found out that she was 'accidently' pregnant, which changed things. Nick had been quite prepared to dump Annabelle after being caught out on the holiday – not that he got round to it. But the pregnancy made him think again. On being given Annabelle's news, he reconsidered his position and thought that he might actually like a fresh start – it seemed a bit rock and roll. He reflected that his life might be similar to Rod Stewart's in this way. True, he couldn't sing a note, but the idea of an extended family worked very well for Rod. He smiled to himself, despite the gravity of the situation. *Now there was one lucky bastard: Britt Eckland, Rachel Hunter, and all the other look-alikes. He had about eight kids by four wives, and they all got on. Yeah, I'll manage just fine with a harem.*

Nick didn't spend too much time thinking about the aspects of his lifestyle that might *not* match Rod's. For example, the millions that got shelled out by the singer in alimony. So, much to Clare's shock and Annabelle's delight, Nick announced that he should do the honourable thing and stand by Annabelle and their expected – or rather unexpected – baby. In fact, honour had nothing to do with Nick's decision; he had lain in bed next to Clare on the night Annabelle had broken the news to him of the baby, and mentally filled in a profit and loss account for the two women, like the true accountant he was.

Annabelle was young - only twenty-five - which was a big plus, as opposed to Clare who was over forty. Again, Rod Steward popped into his head. He had yet to meet a man who had left his wife for an older model. *Well, you just wouldn't, would you? Other than that female director who married a leading man who was still in nappies. What were their names? She was something double-barrelled. She probably had a fixation on John Lennon.*

When he hugged Annabelle he felt that some of her youth and vitality was soaking into his more mature, ageing body. He realised that he hardly hugged Clare nowadays in a romantic way – he just never took the opportunity to. Clare occasionally hugged him, but that was linked to times of crisis; like when her father had died.

These last few years he had noted that Clare had begun to look a bit *worn*, and that was only going to go one way. True, her mother Enid was still looking okay for an oldie – but these things didn't always follow in families. Enid had always played sports; squash when she was young, then tennis, and now bowls. She was very trim, more like Lisa. Clare, on the other hand, had definitely become matronly since their third child, Holly, had been born.

Not like Gabby – oops Annabelle – he quickly corrected himself, his mind drifting to sleep. *Mental note: make sure Annabelle returns to her current sylph-like state once the sprog arrives.* The diet he had suggested to her when she had started work in the office had been very effective, and their affair had knocked pounds off her, apart from her thighs, (they were still disappointingly chunky) but he overlooked that small disappointment.

In the debit column of his mental accounting was mainly Clare and the fact that he couldn't bear to see the hurt in her eyes. He didn't want to spend the next thirty years sitting down to a breakfast of humble pie. *I bloody well don't deserve it, not just for one little mistake,* he convinced himself. *Well, one mistake as far as Clare is aware.* Also in the debit column was the kids. *But kids always bounce back, right?*

Once he had made his decision, he had sat down with the three children to explain about Annie and the baby, and they had taken it really well. They understood that he had to stand by the new baby and be a good dad to it, just like he would continue to be for them. He spun the news in such a way as to place all the blame for the state of affairs fairly and squarely on Annabelle's shoulders.

True, Sally had stormed out at one point, but she had

come around since then. He had promised to take her to stay at the London flat for a shopping weekend. *A few days out in Harrods would soon win her round. He needed to sort that.*

Nick felt that he had been exceedingly generous, offering Clare the family home to provide stability for the kids. But he made it clear right away that she wasn't going to be able to copy the Rod Stewart scenario as far as his wives were concerned and sit at home living off his money.

"Sorry, Clare, but you're going to have to get a proper job now. We haven't got the luxury for you to carry on wasting your degree working in that shop of Brigitte's. Not with another baby on the way."

She had looked up from where she had been sitting on the sofa, frozen with shock. He had announced that he was leaving only the night before. She was still trying to assimilate the idea that the children were going to have a stepbrother or stepsister. Tears started to roll down her cheeks, despite her best efforts to hold them back. It was like trying to stop Niagara from falling.

"But what else can I do?" she had sobbed, frightened at the thought of trying to find a full-time job out in the real world.

Nick had walked into the kitchen to get himself a beer, not interested enough to continue the conversation. That wasn't his problem. He made a mental note to make sure he got Annie back in work as soon as the baby was born. *I'm not making the same mistake with this one. She can get back to work as soon as her maternity leave is over. The promise of a bigger house will keep her sweet.*

* * *

Trying to get a 'proper job', as Nick called it, had not proved to be easy as Clare's computer skills were out of date. After visiting some recruitment agencies, she realised that most jobs needed good IT skills. So, she planned to enrol onto a college course in the January term. In the meantime, she felt grateful for the money she was getting from her shop work and begged Brigitte to give her additional hours where possible.

She had sat one morning crying in the back room while Brigitte made her a cup of strong coffee.

"It shouldn't be allowed," Clare wailed through the tears. "There should be a legal contract that makes parents stay with their children until they are eighteen."

"There is, Clare," replied Brigitte drily. "It's called a Marriage Certificate."

* * *

In the short term, Nick had moved into Annabelle's flat in Oxford, while he and Clare sorted out their finances. He and Annie were looking for a house in central Oxford, so he could walk to work and they could share one car. Traffic in Oxford was such a nightmare that Nick didn't see it as much of a sacrifice. He was looking forward to the move. Oxford would make a nice change from Abingdon. He realised that he had been finding the town a bit provincial.

Luckily for Nick, Clare had always left family finances to him, so she was woefully unaware that he had far more put aside than she could possibly imagine. Clare, being slightly innocent of financial matters, also helped Nick with the divorce proceedings, as she made no demands on his pension. Ben, the divorced colleague of his, had not been so lucky. Ben's wife had made it clear that she was going to get every penny out of him that she could, for as long as she could. *Poor sod. Come retirement, he would still be paying for the first wife.*

Nick was relieved to have his affair finally out in the open, and enjoyed the novelty of introducing Annabelle to Brigitte and the other wives. Of course, some of the wives were a bit sniffy initially, but the men were very impressed with his young conquest.

"Pity she's got up the duff quite so soon," was John's only comment.

Nick was pleased that Brigitte had been welcoming to Annie. He had thought that she might find the situation difficult, as she was such a close friend of Clare's, but in fact she had given the impression that a change of partner was an everyday occurrence. *Good old Brigitte*, he thought gratefully. *Probably because that's what she's used to. Everyone in France has affairs, don't they?* He had another thought. *She knows how to dress smartly and keep trim; she can pass on her tips to Annie.*

As Nick had thought of them meeting, his imagination wandered – as it was so inclined to do - and he lay in bed imagining Brigitte helping to undress Annie in the shop to try on clothes – a steamy porn-fest on which to fall asleep.

* * *

That autumn was also a turning point for Lisa and Phil's marriage. Seeing Clare going through her separation from Nick had made Lisa appreciate what she had in Phil. A bit of long overdue self-analysis over several bottles of wine with friends made her realise that she was quick to criticise but slow to praise, and she felt just a bit guilty about that. Phil was a doting father and a good husband, and had always been faithful, despite having every opportunity to wander because of his job.

Phil's reality was that he actually loved Lisa and his life with her. The random nature of his work made him value the stability of his home life. He saw many steamy relationships kick off on tour, only to disintegrate once real life intruded back on home turf.

The summer job at Abbey Road that had disrupted his summer holiday had led to a permanent job, with an established band that played regularly in London. So, this meant more money and less travelling. His song writing was going well and the band was using some of his material, so he was very happy. There was talk of a recording contract and online streaming, so he was busier than ever.

In fact, Lisa wondered if she had neglected him a little since the children had become such an all-consuming passion. It was time to get back to their early days and join him at some of those concerts he spent his life at. Yes, Lisa would find a babysitter – male, if possible. *I don't want to put temptation in Phil's way. Just look at what Nick has done!* She had not been as sympathetic to Clare's newly-divorced situation as her sister might have hoped.

"Well honestly, Clare, what did you think he was getting up to on those trips to London, for heaven's sake?" She had snapped on one occasion, fed up with Clare's tears. Clare's mouth had dropped open with disbelief.

"I believed what he told me… That he was working… Which he was. How was I to know that he was cheating on me as well?"

Lisa raised her eyes in disbelief. "His problem is that he's too good looking."

"So is Phil, but you don't think he's off having affairs with the entire string section of the orchestra every time he goes away!"

"No, because he's well aware that I'd take him to the cleaners if I ever found out he even looked at another woman. Anyway, he hasn't got that twinkle in his eye that Nick has. You know…" Lisa's voice trailed off.

She couldn't tell Clare that she'd had her suspicions about Nick for some time, but nothing tangible. There was just something about the way he chatted to women, even their own female friends, such as Daphne.

"But I trusted him," wailed Clare plaintively, wanting sympathy but not getting it. She pulled out yet another tissue. *Thank God for aloe, otherwise my nose would be red-raw with all the crying.* "Shouldn't there be trust in a marriage?" she continued pleadingly.

Lisa gave her sister a withering look. *Honestly, for a supposedly intelligent woman she could say some stupid things.* Lisa didn't trust men as far as she could throw them.

Sam was indifferent to his sister's break-up. *At least they're still speaking*, he summed up with a shrug. *It's modern life, isn't it?* He had known that Nick had cheated on Clare in the past – or guessed, at least. Nick would make suggestive comments to John and the other guys: 'Off to my singleton life in London for a couple of days,' he would murmur with a wink. He hadn't actually said it in front of Sam, as he was part of the family, but Sam had heard him talking to the others on more than one occasion. *Oh well, such is married life*, thought Sam.

He hoped that he and Gabby would probably end up tying the knot, but he also knew that if he got a chance to have a brief flirtation, he might be tempted sometime down the line. *Just don't get caught, eh?* He reminded himself.

Despite having known divorced couples and imagined it happening to herself and Nick, Clare had never dreamt of the dramatic impact it would have on her group of friends. She had only worried about the impact it would have on the children.

She was beginning to feel like a pariah. She and Nick had socialised so much with other couples that she had made very little time for the few single friends she had outside of their gang. The fact that all their children also socialised together made it even more comfortable for them to meet up, and of course the children were all still friends. She had never considered the decrease in the number of invitations that would occur because of the divorce, but that had already started to happen.

During the immediate aftermath of the separation she had not wanted to see anyone. She was so devastated that she sat crying for hours, too miserable to socialise. Gradually, she had taken stock of her single status and tried to start her new life as a divorcee – *horrible word*, she hated it – and slowly realised that the gang now embraced Nick and Annabelle, and not her.

She thought back to a strange conversation she'd had

with Daphne, not long after Nick had moved out. Daphne had insisted on taking her out to lunch to cheer her up.

"After all, darling, you might as well get used to the fact that you're on your own. He won't be back - not with the baby on the way," she had stated in her usual, blunt manner.

When they were seated at the restaurant, Daphne had insisted that Clare have something substantial to eat. "You need fattening up, Poppet. No good wasting away over him," she said, coaxing her to order something filling.

To please her, Clare had ordered a pizza that she didn't want. She only managed to eat two slices. *Never mind. I'll take the rest home for Toby.* That was when she remembered that Toby and the girls were going to their father's that night, and hot tears of self-pity sprung up in her eyes. Daphne had noticed, and reached over to give her hand a sympathetic squeeze. Clare wondered if she should start on the happy pills that her friends kept telling her to take. *It would only be for a while.*

"Oh, you poor thing! It's so hard, isn't it? Remember, I've been there," Daphne cooed consolingly.

In fact, Daphne had sailed through two divorces, but they both had been of her choosing, with her walking out and leaving the husbands staring after her speedily receding back.

"Nick's such a bastard, treating you like this," she had continued. "Mind you, it was inevitable…" She stopped when she saw the puzzled look Clare gave her.

"What on earth do you mean?" asked Clare, wiping away her tears.

"Oh, nothing…" she trailed off. *God, Brigitte was right! The poor cow had no idea what Nick was really like.*

"No, honestly, Daphne. What do you mean by that?" Clare repeated.

"Nothing at all! He's just the type, that's all," she blustered.

"Daphne, do you know something I don't?" asked Clare slowly, giving up on any attempt to finish her food.

Daphne looked down at her plate, avoiding eye contact. She was confident that the occasional couplings she'd had with Nick were still secret. She felt no guilt. *Out of sight, out of mind*, was her motto. Life was much more fun when you were discreet about these things and didn't get emotionally involved. *After all; it's only sex. You just have to be discreet.*

"Of course not," she lied. "I just mean – well – he's awfully attractive. Too good looking for his own good..." She quickly changed the subject. "Anyway, let's order some pudding. That will cheer you up." So they did, and it didn't. The lunch that had meant to cheer her up, left her sadder and more confused than when she had walked into the bistro.

Since then, Clare had sensed that perhaps her friends knew something about Nick's past that she didn't. But nobody was talking. So much for old friends! At that moment Clare thought that life could not be more miserable.

19

Another New Year

It was not a good start to the New Year. Clare had been woken early on New Year's morning by the puppy jumping on her bed at 7 am, disturbing her sleep.

After losing Pepper in the dramatic way they had, the children had been distraught. The easiest way to deal with the loss had been to buy another puppy.

Clare had phoned the same breeder that they had bought Pepper from and, by chance, she had a six-month-old golden cocker spaniel that had not been sold. Clare was pleased in more ways than one – she could quite happily miss the first three months of toilet training required for younger puppies, *and* they got a new companion. She had taken the children to pick the new dog up in September and, after many heated and protracted discussions that would have done credit to delegates of the United Nations, they had decided on a name. Holly had eventually won the honour of naming the puppy, after his golden coat.

"He's toffee-coloured, so of course he should be called Toffee," she had insisted. "We gave Pepper his name because he was so black, so we should do the same with this one," she declared, hugging the silky bundle to her chest.

As Clare gave the little puppy his breakfast and put him into the garden for his morning visit to the trees and shrubs, she briefly thought of Pepper, who had never been found. She was so grateful to have Toffee. *At least I've got someone to cuddle*, she thought sadly. *Right*. She put on a stern expression. *Back in the present. Those kinds of thoughts won't help me get through today.*

She gave her reflection a stare of disapproval, and went upstairs to dress. Throwing on her clothes – grey, to match her mood – she thought about her New Year's Eve, spent at home, alone. To her intense dismay, their gang had accepted Annabelle into their midst. Although they hadn't dropped Clare, being single now, she couldn't bear turning up to events where Nick and *her* were invited. She just could not spend the evening watching her husband of twenty years with his new girlfriend - a girlfriend many years her junior at that!

Last night there had been the usual big party - this year at Duncan and Deb's rambling Victorian villa. Their three children had gone to be with their friends, along with Nick and Annabelle. Debs had called around especially to invite Clare, explaining that, as Duncan and Nick had been in school together, he couldn't possibly not invite Nick.

"You know what these men are like, darling. They're all just big boy scouts," she had said with a laugh. Clare had not joined in the laughter. This was the hardest cut of all – being *the ex-wife*.

What was even worse than missing New Year's Eve with all her friends, was that she would also be missing the traditional open house event on New Year's Day at Brigitte and John's. It seemed a betrayal of Brigitte's friendship with Clare that Nick and Annabelle had also been invited there for brunch. Sally, Toby, and Holly had spent the night before sleeping at Annabelle and Nick's flat, so that they could all head off the next morning to spend New Year's Day as usual at John and Brigitte's.

Brigitte, to her credit, had been suitably embarrassed about inviting Nick and Annabelle. She had put off making the difficult call to her old friend, but had finally made it after a fortifying glass of chilled Chablis. She knew that she was being a coward, as they had been working together in the shop all day. She reluctantly picked the phone up and explained to Clare that it was John who had insisted on inviting Nick and his new partner, as he and Nick were such old friends. *So much for seeking solace with close friends!* thought Clare as she ended the call.

To be fair to Brigitte, but unbeknownst to Clare, she'd not been party to the row that had taken place between John and Brigitte immediately prior to the phone call. John had been unmoveable.

"Of course I'm inviting Nick!" he had barked. "I've known him for over twenty years. It wouldn't be the same without him around; everyone loves him."

"Well, I've known Clare nearly as long," replied Brigitte. "And I know that she will be really hurt if Nick turns up with his new woman."

"Too bad! I've already invited him – so tough!" With that abrupt close to the conversation John marched out of the kitchen, slamming the door for good measure.

"Of course, you are invited too, Clare," Brigitte had gushed over the phone, almost stumbling over her words in her haste to get the call over with.

Clare fought back her tears. She knew that she would hate being there on her own, but perversely wanted Nick and Annabelle not to be there either. Brigitte spoke again, interrupting the long silence.

"Of course, the children will want to see their friends…?" Her voice trailed off with embarrassment. It was half apology, half question.

Still, Clare didn't know about any of this, to her Brigitte had turned her back on her. So, Clare had spent the remainder of New Year's Eve with fresh determination to change her job. The idea of spending all her time with Brigitte after this stab in the back would be too difficult. She had also become a cause for gossip, and hated acquaintances coming into the shop and asking how she was 'bearing up'.

Sally was the only one of the three children who seemed to understand how hard the New Year festivities were for Clare. Just as her father's car drove up to collect them all, she turned to her mother. "Do you want me to stay at home with you, Mum?" she had asked at the last minute, suddenly realising that her mother was going to be left alone for what – in the past – had always been such a fun-filled couple of days.

"No, sweetheart, you're alright," she replied, trying to keep her voice bright and cheerful. "You know I could have arranged something if I'd wanted to, but I'll enjoy watching Jools Holland on TV," she lied. "I'll be able to hear him for once, without all the shouting." It was a feeble joke, but it managed to keep her voice light.

Of course, once she had been left on her own, she had regretted turning down the limited offers that had been made by her single friends for her to join them. She had a quick cry, hugging Toffee. She wondered how she could have ended up in such a lonely situation. She wanted to phone her mother for some sympathy, but in the end decided not to, only because it would make her mother worry about her.

Enid had been up to stay on more than one occasion since Nick's departure. She was desperately sorry to see Clare so unhappy, but felt powerless to help. She had met Annabelle briefly when she and Nick had turned up to collect the children, and felt very proud of herself that she had managed not to slap the little bitch across her pretty little face. She had several friends who had been through the same situation, and had to watch their grandchildren deal with the upheaval in their lives.

One of the positive outcomes of the divorce, fortunately, was that the children had not been as upset as she had expected. They had so many friends in school who had divorced parents that, when they had turned up to tell their story of woe, they had mainly been met with shrugs of indifference, as if to say, "You think that's bad; you should hear what's going on in my life."

Late on New Year's Eve, Clare had poured herself a glass of good Merlot to welcome in the New Year (Nick had left his expensive wines - too ashamed to collect them when he had picked up all his clothes). *At least he feels some guilt,* thought Clare as she toasted Toffee and reflected on the past year. Jools Holland played in the corner of the room, watched but not enjoyed.

What hurt her most – almost as much as Nick leaving her – was how all her friends had accepted the new *status quo*. The mistress was 'great fun', apparently; and this from her sister, Lisa, of all people! Lisa had been very loyal to Clare, but – just as with Brigitte and John – Phil was an old friend of Nick's.

So, gradually, Clare felt that she was becoming the outsider of the group, not Nick. *Not that I want this to be a competition between us*, she had thought generously. But it had somehow become one.

Right, no more mulling over last night, she told herself severely as she pulled on wellies and a warm coat to walk the new puppy. She trudged along the towpath, trying not to think of the buzz that would be happening in Brigitte's kitchen. *At least the children will be having fun,* she consoled herself. She looked up, hoping to see blue skies, but there was only low cloud the colour of pewter. *Even the trees look miserable*, she thought, as she trudged along. The lines of meandering trees along the Thames were lush and verdant in the spring and summer months, but at this time of year were as bare and barren as the pylons that strutted across the fields from nearby Didcot Power Station. *At least it's not raining yet*, she told herself, determined to think positively.

When she returned to her empty house, she looked at the time on the wall clock. It was still only nine-thirty. *How am I going to fill my day?*

She wandered upstairs to her bedroom and stood

looking into the room as if she had never seen it before. This had been her marital bedroom for twenty years and was unchanged since Nick had moved out, other than his now empty wardrobe and chest of drawers. She had not had the heart to use them since he had gone.

Until now! Today was the day!

She put on the local talk radio station to keep her company, and flung open all of the wardrobes. She decided to move all her dresses into Nick's old wardrobe, and leave her separates where they were. As she started to sort through the rails of clothes, she threw three dresses onto the bed that Nick had chosen for her that she had never liked. They were short, bright and silky, with low-cut cleavages that revealed more of her ample bosom than she cared to expose.

She thought back to when she had last worn the red dress. He had been lying on the bed watching her getting ready for a night out together, suggesting what she would wear as she wandered round in a towel.

"What about that red underwear I bought for your birthday?" he suggested. "I haven't seen you in them yet." He only ever bought black and red lace.

She had reluctantly pulled the set out of the drawer, and her face had fallen. The bra looked lacy and itchy, and the briefs were a thong. When Clare was growing up, thongs were called g-strings, and the only women that wore them were strippers. She had put them on, feeling overweight and underdressed, and Nick had appeared delighted.

"That's more like it," he had murmured. "Come over here and let's see how quickly they come off."

"Not now," she had shrieked. "There's no time." She had slipped into her shiny dress before he made a grab for her.

The memory gave Clare mixed emotions; sadness that Nick was no longer there on the bed, and pleasure at what she planned to do with the hated bras and pants.

She opened her underwear drawer and pulled out all the skimpy sets that Nick had bought her over the years. She skipped down to the laundry room and found a large plastic bag. She took the stairs back up to the bedroom, two at a time. Back in her bedroom, she shoved the satin dresses and lacy underwear in the bag, ready to take to *Oxfam* on her way to work the next morning.

She turned to the drawers of her dressing table. At the back of her jewellery drawer lay her wedding, engagement, and eternity rings, exactly where she had flung them after a particularly unhappy comment from Nick. He had been picking up the children and she was not going out, so had not changed from her comfy pyjamas.

When the children were safely stowed in the car, he turned to her and said sincerely, "I know you won't mind me saying, but you must take care not to let yourself go just because there isn't a man around."

With that, he had given her a peck on the cheek and driven off. *Bastard!*

Just thinking of that made Clare pink with anger. She looked down at the unfamiliarly bare fingers of her left hand, with the pale band of skin on her ring finger where her wedding ring had always been. She had planned to leave her rings to Sally, as the oldest daughter, just as Enid had said she would do for her. But what did they count for now? Instead of symbolising a happy marriage, they were just any old bits of gold and diamonds that you could find in any shop window on the high street. She took them out of the drawer and put them on her finger. She was not one for expensive jewellery, so had not traded up for expensive new models as the years went by; these were the real deal. Yet another dream shattered by the divorce.

She took them off and held them in the palm of her hand, wondering what to do with them. *What to do, what to do?* Suddenly, she had an idea. She would take them to a goldsmith in town and have the gold made into a thick band, set with the birthstones of each of the children, which she would wear on her ring finger. There might even be some money left over from the diamonds to spend on something – anything. Her mood instantly switched from morose to delight as she planned this meaningful and forward-looking activity. Continually contemplating the past had been such an easy trap to fall into.

She dropped the rings onto the dresser and opened the next drawer. There were three unopened bottles of Chanel No. 5 at the back. She hadn't had the heart to tell Nick she had gone off the scent after Toby had been born. Taste in perfumes can change over time, but he was always so sentimental about it. He would watch her open the familiar-shaped parcel and say, "In memory of our first Christmas together, darling." She had continued to wear it, out of duty rather than anything else. Well, not any longer! Here were three ready-made presents to re-gift to her friends. The two opened ones would do to keep her shoes smelling fresh. She would go and choose a new perfume the next time she was shopping in Oxford, which would symbolise the new her.

After lunch, she sat at the computer and logged onto *figleaves.com* – an underwear retailer. She spent a happy afternoon scrolling through screens of underwear, ignoring all the lacy sets, and finally selecting some colourful lycra ones with stripes and polka dots that appealed far more to her sense of style. Her recent loss of weight meant that she had gone down a bra size, so she could justify the expense. She smiled with satisfaction as she added them to her basket. *Not a thong or bit of lace in sight.*

20

A Different Easter

It was Easter, and Clare had the long Bank Holiday weekend ahead of her without the children. On the Saturday morning she woke with a feeling of pleasure as she looked around her bedroom. It did not look particularly different, but the knowledge that the contents of the wardrobes and drawers were all hers now lifted her spirits. She enjoyed the new feeling of having space for all her clothes.

Over the past weeks she had moved around the lighter pieces of furniture, and put up photos of the children on the bedroom walls. Nick had never liked their photos up in the bedroom. It was becoming her room now, rather than hers and Nick's.

* * *

The children had gone to stay with Nick and Annabelle for the weekend. The couple now lived off Woodstock Road just north of Oxford city centre. The house they had moved into was a small Victorian semi which Nick was not too impressed with after living in the spacious family home in Abingdon.

He planned to upgrade as soon as finances allowed. He needed a bigger place for the kids, apart from anything else. They liked staying with their father as they could walk into the city centre from the house.

Annabelle, however, loved their first home together after her pokey flat and spent all her spare time on home improvements, with particular attention being spent on decorating the nursery. She would sit on the nursing chair she had bought, and try to imagine life as a new mother.

Looking after Nick's children did not count as mothering to Annabelle, as Holly – the youngest – was already eight years old. She couldn't imagine how she would manage with the baby and her new stepchildren, which was probably just as well. The new baby was due the following month, so Annabelle had left work for her maternity leave, forcing Nick to find a replacement secretary. She had joked with him:

"I hope my replacement is fat and forty!"

You can hope all you want, thought Nick. Her replacement was a twenty-two-year-old graduate with a fine mind and an even finer body. *What was the saying? When you marry the mistress you create a vacancy.*

* * *

Arrangements for the Easter weekend included the annual barbecue at John and Brigitte's, but the unusually dull weather and forecasts of rain had caused a change in plans.

John had told Brigitte about his decision in no uncertain terms. "I'm not standing freezing my bollocks off while everybody else stays inside in the warm. Sod that for a game of soldiers! I'll buy a large rib of beef and barbecue it in the morning, and we'll serve it up indoors. The party will just have to be different this year."

Different in more ways than one, thought Brigitte, missing the companionship of Clare, who continued to avoid functions that Nick and Annabelle attended.

* * *

Clare had thought of driving down to Wales to stay with her mother for the long weekend, but Enid was off to Ireland for a bowls tour. She tried to sound contrite on the phone.

"Sorry, darling. I'd love to have you here, but I can't let the team down. We're doing really well in the league."

As she proceeded to list the successes of the Ladies' Bowls Team (Veterans), Clare knew that she wouldn't want it any other way. But it would have been nice to have her mother making a fuss of her. *Oh well, I'll just have to find something to do locally.* She looked out of the window at the threatening clouds. Gardening was definitely out of the question.

Once she had finished her early morning cup of tea, she pulled on her dog-walking coat and set off to walk along the Thames tow path. The promised heavy rain had not descended as yet, although the black scudding clouds looked ready to empty their cargo of rain at any moment. She decided to walk along the Thames Path down to Culham, the next village south of Abingdon, and – if she was feeling brave enough – call into the pub for a drink and a warm meal before heading back. There was usually a large log fire burning in an inglenook, something that always lifted her spirits. She had never liked walking into pubs on her own, but this was one of the ways that she was dealing with being a, *dreaded word,* singleton. She had thought that this was a term only used for twenty-somethings, but the alternative – divorcee – was even more depressing.

As she strolled along the riverbank she made a mental checklist of all the good aspects of her life since Nick had left, to try and cheer herself up. One positive change in Clare's life was her new job. She had visited a local employment agency in January and had been offered a low-paid admin job with a local company. As it was full-time it paid more than her salary from *The Clothes Horse* but, more importantly, there were opportunities to progress within the company. They had a large number of employees, and she enjoyed meeting them during the course of her working day. In this way she was gradually making a new circle of friends.

She had also started her computing course and was pleased to find it well within her capabilities. She was sorry she hadn't done it years ago and was looking forward to the exam, and to the qualification that she could add to her CV.

As she thought about work and studies, she smiled to herself at how well she was coping with her new life. She stuffed her hands in her coat pockets and marched along resolutely, determined to make it to the pub, and hopefully before the anticipated cloudburst. The alternative was sitting at home moping in front of the TV.

Suddenly, Toffee started barking frantically from further along the tow path. He had seen a large crow. It was innocently sitting on a low branch, watching the world going by, not expecting a young pup of very little intelligence to come bowling along. The bird gave Toffee a disdainful look, a loud 'caw', and flapped noisily into the air. Clare called Toffee away, but he took no notice and carried on barking. As the yapping continued, a man stepped off a narrow boat moored alongside the towpath. Narrow boats were a familiar sight along the river banks here. His boat was painted in the traditional ornate style, with the name *Steady Eddy* picked out on the side in bright gold and green paint, a welcome touch of colour in the monochrome landscape. He looked at Toffee, then across to Clare, and smiled.

"What's all the noise about?"

Clare explained about the crow, but the bird had now flown and was nowhere to be seen.

"Heading anywhere in particular?" he asked her.

Clare paused. She had planned this walk to be alone, and didn't know whether she wanted the company of a stranger. On the other hand, he had a friendly face, and was smiling expectantly down at her. A year ago she would have thought him forward and walked past with a frosty smile, but that was then, and this was now. *In for a penny…*

"I'm walking a couple of miles down the towpath to a village pub." Clare pointed in the direction in which she intended to walk.

"Mind if I join you?" asked the stranger. "I'm not from around here, and I fancy a drink myself. These boats are cold at this time of year, even with a fire burning."

She could smell the bitter smoke that was curling up from a chimney at the rear of the boat. *Goodness*, she thought, *am I being picked up?* She didn't know one way or the other, but decided that any company was preferable to her own right then.

"Yes, company would be good." She smiled, and felt light-hearted. As she spoke, he turned in the direction that Clare was headed and fell into step alongside her. Together they continued the walk, chatting as they strolled.

"I like the name of your boat," she remarked. "How did you choose it?"

"It's what my friends call me – Steady Eddie – because I can always be relied on in a crisis, and we had a few of those in our younger days! I just changed the spelling to give it a nautical spin."

Clare liked the sound of that – someone who could be relied on in a crisis. He went on to explain that he was a technical editor that he lived on the boat all year round, and that he was on his way to Oxford for the summer. He had no plans after that.

As they walked along side by side, there was a break in the clouds and a shaft of weak winter sun broke through the passing stormy clouds. By the time they reached the pub, introductions had been made and, just for a fleeting moment, Clare was able to set aside thoughts of the past. As they entered the cosy bar, she realised that life in the future was going to be different and – just maybe – it wouldn't be all that bad.

Acknowledgements

Many thanks to Ffion Bartley, my ferocious Editrix. Additional thanks to John Holton, my forensic proof reader. Any errors that remain after they finished with the text are down to me.

Thanks also to Fiona Cringle for advising on the dog rescue. Those years as an auxiliary coastguard were not wasted!

Thanks to Jess Bartley for suggesting that Sophie clings to her mobile phone!

Finally, to my friends and family: some of the locations and settings may be familiar, but if you think you are featured in the story – you're not!

About Cal Bartley

Cal has worked for many years in education, specialising in literacy and managing challenging behaviour. Since then she has been involved in specialist communications tutoring and coaching.

She has taught creative writing, which led to her writing short stories. She was the winner of the Onion Custard Short Story Competition 2015,

Cal has three daughters and lives in the seaside town of Penarth, South Wales, with her husband. She loves to travel, and the fact that one of her girls is working in Rome gives her an excuse to make regular visits to Italy. The other two girls live in and near London, so regular excursions are also made to the capital. Cal likes to attend festivals in her camper van.

This is her first novel.

Connect with Cal:

     www.catalystcoachingtraining.co.uk
     cal_bartley@msn.com
     Twitter: @CarolynBartley
     Find her on Facebook: *Cal Bartley*

ND - #0114 - 270225 - C0 - 203/127/9 - PB - 9781909129887 - Matt Lamination